"What are y

The voice was deep, harsh concern tightly packed in those six words. Stunned at the sudden ferocity, she raised her hand holding the tablet, trying to defuse his tone with a smile. Her eyes scanned the person standing at the door and widened as she recognized who stood in front of her. Dr. Handsome.

His jaw was taut, but beneath his standoffish stance she spotted the man that smiled with such kindness on the covers of magazines. And going by what she saw as she let her eyes drift down, those magazines could be medical journals or a swimsuit cover. He wouldn't look misplaced in either. The sheer masculinity commanded the room with no effort.

"You're Dr. Henderson," she said. To her eternal relief, her voice didn't crack. She only got one chance at making a good impression, and the way his eyes narrowed made her believe that chance hung by a thin thread. "I'm Emma Santos, the new anesthesiologist."

Dear Reader,

This story has been with me for over two years and underwent quite the metamorphosis to get to this point where you are now reading it. Mark and Emma's story started as little more than some disconnected scenes in my head, and the—now no longer idle—fantasy of bringing this story out there for people to read it. It still seems strange to think about it as I'm typing this.

Romance stories have always held a special place in my heart, and in recent years I've been obsessed with the diversity that has started to become more and more the norm across the genre. To see that my people could be the front and center of the stories I read was so inspiring that I had to try to be part of representing Latinx culture in the romance genre.

Coming from a long line of medical professionals, there was no better way for me to honor my heritage than to craft a story where a strong Latin woman is the protagonist, along with her swoon-worthy hero, to sweep her off her feet.

Luana

FALLING FOR HER
OFF-LIMITS BOSS

LUANA DaROSA

MEDICAL
ROMANCE

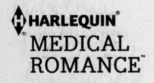

HARLEQUIN®
MEDICAL
ROMANCE™

Recycling programs
for this product may
not exist in your area.

ISBN-13: 978-1-335-40916-4

Falling for Her Off-Limits Boss

Copyright © 2022 by Luana DaRosa

This edition published by arrangement with Harlequin Books S.A.

For questions and comments about the quality of this book,
please contact us at CustomerService@Harlequin.com.

Harlequin Enterprises ULC
22 Adelaide St. West, 41st Floor
Toronto, Ontario M5H 4E3, Canada
www.Harlequin.com

Printed in U.S.A.

Once at home in sunny Brazil, **Luana DaRosa** has since lived on three different continents, though her favourite romantic location remains the tropical places of Latin America. When not typing away at her latest romance novel or reading about love, Luana is either crocheting, buying yarn she doesn't need or chasing her bunnies around her house. She lives with her partner in the northeast of England.

Falling for Her Off-Limits Boss
is Luana DaRosa's debut title for Harlequin

Visit the Author Profile page at Harlequin.com.

For Alex, my partner in crime in everything I do. This is as much yours as it is mine.

CHAPTER ONE

ALEXANDER ATTANO MEMORIAL. Emma's heart skipped a beat as she read the letters, pulling into the car park of the hospital that would be her new temporary home. With four boxes containing her belongings and a wounded heart, she had left San Francisco to flee from the chaos her ex-boyfriend Rob had brought to her.

Emma closed her eyes and shook away the dark clouds forming in her head. She had to remind herself that she had made it. She'd got out. Her life was her own again. And she would make the best out of her time spent as a locum tenens anaesthetist.

What better way of spending the summer than in Chicago, learning from the world-renowned Mark Henderson? Emma's heart skipped a beat when her thoughts drifted towards the famous surgeon who worked at the hospital.

When she entered the building the reception area was spread out right in front of her, with a middle-aged woman sitting behind the counter talking to a man wearing a white coat and dark green scrubs. The receptionist laughed at something the doctor said, waving her hand at him.

'I will page you as soon as they arrive,' Emma heard her say as she approached the desk, her eyes running over this man who would be the first colleague she got to meet.

His dark brown hair was just long enough to be styled, but the way he wore it looked wild and untamed, matching the five o'clock shadow covering his cheeks. As he turned around she caught his glance, the friendly spark in his hazel eyes showing the friendship he shared with the receptionist.

A shiver trickled down her spine as his gaze locked onto hers. His face was familiar. She recognised him. But who was he? How could she forget the name belonging to such a handsome face? *Wait, was he...?*

Emma caught her thoughts before she let them go any further. In front of her stood her first co-worker. There were many words she could use to describe him, and handsome shouldn't be one of them. After Rob, she wasn't going to let herself regard her colleagues in any other way than with professional courtesy. The moment their personal lives had become at odds with their professional ones he had conveniently forgotten what a true partnership looked like. Even their slightest disagreements at work had become an issue of huge proportions once they got home.

It had taught Emma a valuable lesson. Work and private life should touch as little as possible.

'Thanks, Becky, you are a star,' the handsome doctor said, and walked off. But not without looking at Emma again, smiling as he passed her.

Her stomach lurched, and she held her breath for a moment. As he disappeared, Becky waved at her to step closer.

'Hello, dear, how can I help you?' she asked, the friendly glow in her eyes remaining and setting Emma at ease.

'My name is Emma Santos. I'm the new anaesthesiologist starting today in Oncology. HR told me to sign in at the front desk.'

Becky's smile widened. 'Why, yes, I've been expecting you. Welcome to Attano Memorial! I have your badge right here. Let me call someone from HR to sort you out for today. Too bad Dr Henderson just left, or he could have taken you with him.'

Emma snapped her head around, wanting to catch a glimpse of the man mentioned, but he had already disappeared.

'So it *was* Mark Henderson!' Her pulse quickened, and Emma slipped a hand inside her tote bag, retrieving the medical journal she'd brought from home. Mark Henderson smiled up at her from its cover. The unmoving image didn't even begin to do him justice.

'Yes, Mark leads the oncology department. But his focus lies within surgery.' Becky was looking at the screen in front of her, oblivious to Emma's amazement. She put a key card on the counter as she picked up the phone, dialled a number.

Emma picked up the badge, examining it. The excitement bubbling up within her was subdued by a nervous energy rearing its head from the pit of her stomach. In her new role as locum anaesthetist she would work side by side with Dr Henderson, a fact that already made her stomach lurch.

She had read all his research on pain management for different cancer treatments, and yearned for the chance to contribute her own knowledge to it. The devastation wrought by chemotherapy often required a fresh approach to traditional pain medication, and Dr Henderson was one of the top surgeons in that area. He was the reason she was most excited to start her role here. His proximity had set her nerve-ends on fire. Now she understood why. She'd been inches away from the man she'd once thought might save her mother.

When her mother had first been diagnosed with Gardner Syndrome, a rare type of hereditary cancer, Emma had read every single piece of research around the disease. She'd wanted to understand the odds her mother was fighting against. Back then she had just started her second year of med school in San Francisco, which had made the different texts and studies a lot more accessible to her.

While not specifically focusing on Gardner Syndrome, Dr Henderson's research looked into types of aggressive colon cancer and how different treatments could be adapted to any specific case. His breakthroughs had given Emma hope that her mother might be able to get through the disease alive. A vain hope, as she now knew, but a few years ago she'd hung on to it with everything she had. To save her mother and also to save herself.

With a hereditary disease like Gardner Syndrome, chances were that her mother had passed the condition on to Emma. A potential diagnosis hung over her head every day, just waiting to drop. After her mother's diagnosis her father had urged her to get tested for the gene mutation, to determine whether she had the disease as well, but every time Emma had come close to taking the test she'd pulled out.

First she had told herself that she needed to

focus on her mother. She didn't want to burden her with the thought that she might have passed this disease to her only child. But even after her death Emma hadn't found the heart to find out the truth. Her father, along with her aunts, uncles and cousins, regularly teamed up to inundate her with messages and phone calls about having the test. She knew that eventually she would have to find out. For the sake of her future children, she needed to know.

When things had started looking more serious with Rob she had been so close to getting the test, wanting to know how it would affect their future. A future that was no longer.

Emma's mouth went dry and she took those stray thoughts, stuffing them back into the box where they belonged. This was her fresh start, after having her heart and soul crushed by the man who had promised to love her. She yearned to learn and thrive. And put all that behind her.

Emma shook her head, straightened her shoulders, and found her smile again as the HR representative came to pick her up.

'Try to get a bit more sleep.'

Mark smiled at his patient as he approached the door, giving him a small wave before he left for the nurses' desk. He hadn't meant to wake him up, simply wanting to check up on him before his regular shift began. This was one of the happier cases Mark had worked on and a rare sight in the oncology department. The cancer had been at its early stages, but in a tricky position. Difficult enough that the oncologist had asked Mark to do the surgery.

Not that he minded the more complicated cases. Everyone who needed his attention got it. From the moment he got a patient file up to the point when the patient walked out of this hospital, he considered them all his responsibility, and his colleagues were aware that he expected the same from everyone in his department.

He took down a few notes on the patient's condition and headed for the nurses' station. Theresa, the oncology department's head nurse, stood behind the desk, so engrossed in whatever was on her clipboard that she did not register his presence.

He cleared his throat, but it didn't grab her attention. 'Good morning, Theresa,' he said, with a slight smile that grew larger when she jumped, laying her hand over her heart and breathing a sigh of relief.

'Goodness! Stop sneaking up on me,' she said in a playful tone, rolling her eyes at him when he shrugged.

'I didn't mean to scare you. You were busy with your work, I swear.' Placing his arms on the counter, he leaned in. 'What are you working on?'

'I'm checking the schedule changes for today before I put it up on the board. With our new anaesthesiologist arriving yesterday, we can stop stealing them from other departments.'

Her words caught him by surprise. The new anaesthesiologist had started yesterday? The locum position was to cover the maternity leave of their own anaesthesiologist. She had only left last week, and he hadn't expected anyone to arrive so soon. Christine herself had only switched to the oncology department a couple of weeks ago. Now he needed to train a new doctor from scratch, when he knew exactly who would have been the perfect person for the job.

His left hand contracted into a fist and he glanced down. It had taken him a long time after the funeral to take off his ring. Even now, close to two years after Claire's passing, the weight of the wedding band sometimes still lingered on his finger.

She had been an incredible source of knowledge and comfort to him when they were working together on their cancer research projects. Then she'd been diagnosed with cancer herself. But her prognosis was looking good. Mark had thought they would spend the rest of their lives together. Until her oncologist had informed him that she was taking a turn for the worse.

Mark had already started his own work rotation at that point, since Claire had been headed towards remission. He wished he could say that no one in the department had seen it coming, that her demise had come overnight and blindsided them all. But the truth was far worse. He'd missed her last moments in life because he had been too busy trying to find the breakthrough in cancer treatment that they had both been working on for the last years. He'd been trying so hard to save himself the pain of losing her that he'd lost sight of what it meant to be an adequate husband to his dying wife.

Mark had promised he would be there for her when she died, but in the end he hadn't been.

The darkness that came with memories of his late wife was a familiar one, and the guilt of her death rested on his shoulders alone. It wrapped around him like a cocoon, blocking out any other emotion.

'What can you tell me about the new person?' he asked, to distract himself from his inner turmoil.

His question made Theresa lift her eyes from her clipboard. 'Why do you want to know? Don't think I haven't heard your complaints about having a locum anaesthesiologist hired.

But you know we desperately need someone. Dr Anderson won't be back for another several weeks and you already scared away two replacements.'

Mark clasped his hands above his heart, feigning pain as he grunted, drawing a laugh from Theresa's lips. 'You think I'm the reason the new hires left? You wound me.'

'If the shoe fits…'

'I'm making sure they're committed to our service. With our patients, stability is one of the most important things. If they see a different doctor each time, how will they develop trust in us? I know it's not their fault, but that doesn't change the fact that our patients need consistency.'

'Her name is Emma Santos, and she came here from a private practice in San Francisco.' Theresa sighed. 'She has already arrived and is settling in for her first surgery this morning. You have one surgery with her later on—a tumour resection—so you can get used to each other then. I saw her pass by just moments ago. You should introduce yourself.'

Mark raised an eyebrow at Theresa's words. She had arrived early on her first day. That was an attitude he could appreciate. 'I'll do just that.'

Mark set high standards for the care of his patients. Those standards were responsible for his department dwarfing the national average recovery time. The last thing he needed was a stranger by his side, poking and prodding at those standards. Compromising patient care was unacceptable, and he expected his colleagues to be on top of their game.

Despite his own shortcomings, the team looking after Claire had been an invaluable resource to lean on. He'd become familiar with everyone on her team, drawing comfort from their experience. They knew everything there was to know when it came to consoling patients and their families alike. That wasn't something a doctor from a private practice could possibly know.

What was the chief of surgery thinking? Mark frowned. Locum doctors were no more than tourists, wanting to see the world while practising medicine. He had met enough of them to know he didn't like these kinds of mercenary physicians.

But, since he was stuck with this temporary colleague, he planned on ensuring she understood what kind of service he ran.

Emma had arrived early for her second day at Attano Memorial—the first day she would actually get to do surgery. After announcing her arrival at Reception yesterday, she had spent almost all her time sitting in the HR office, signing contracts and waivers about the hospital's safety procedures, code of conduct and other documents requiring her signature. After that, the HR assistant had given her the grand tour of the hospital, introducing her to some key figures.

It had disappointed her when Mark Henderson hadn't been one of the important people for her to meet. He was the reason she'd come here rather than going back to Brazil for a couple of weeks before starting her fellowship—a choice that hadn't come easy to her. Between med school, internship and residency, Emma hadn't had time to make the trip back to Brazil to see her family. Her cousins called her often, filling her in on the latest gossip in the Santos clan, but it made her long to see her family again.

When things had started looking serious with Rob, she had tried to convince him to take a trip with her and meet her family. But somehow it had never been the right moment. Business had been more important, and he'd refused to lose any appointments, guilting her into staying even when she had planned on taking a trip without him.

Because of that she hadn't been back to Brazil since her mother's funeral. But this opportunity had been too good to pass up, and when she'd called her father to tell him about it he had been beyond excited for her to learn from the best there was. He had always been her biggest supporter.

After stuffing her things into her locker, Emma found the whiteboard the HR assistant had mentioned would hold the surgery schedule, and when her eyes found her name on the board she couldn't help but smile. Her first surgery would be in ninety minutes with a Dr Shearer.

She typed the patient file number on the board into the tablet she had got at the nurses' station. The patient file soon loaded, including all the history and notes from the oncologist.

Nodding to herself, Emma glanced at the board again. Three surgeries were scheduled in OR One, her operating room for the day. One of them in the afternoon with Dr Henderson. The prospect of working with him both excited and terrified her in equal measure. His reputation was for being strict, but that that came from a deep care for his patients.

She entered the OR and glanced around, letting the gravity of the moment sink in. The room was much larger than the operating theatres she had got used to during her residency.

Rob had convinced her to join him at his private practice rather than continue her residency at the hospital. She had believed him when he'd told her how much better it would be for her training. How *romantic* it would be for them to work together as a couple. When in truth he'd only wanted her close to him to exert control on everything she did, both at work and outside of it. Now she felt unprepared—deprived of the experience she could only have got in a hospital environment.

Emma swallowed to calm the insecurities bubbling up. She picked up the tablet and opened the checklist she'd written last night in preparation. She needed to be sure that everything was where it should be. Starting with the item at the top of the list, she circled the whole OR, checking every item, before a voice interrupted her.

'What are you doing in here?'

The voice was deep, with harsh concern tightly packed in those six words. Stunned at the sudden ferocity, she raised the hand holding the tablet, trying to defuse his tone with a smile. Her eyes scanned the person standing at the door and widened as she recognised who stood in front of her.

Mark Henderson. Dr Handsome.

His jaw was taut, but beneath his stand-off-ish stance she spotted the man who smiled with such kindness on the covers of magazines. And, going by what she saw as she let her eyes drift down, those magazines could be medical journals or a swimsuit special. He wouldn't look misplaced in either. His sheer masculinity commanded the room with no effort.

'You're Dr Henderson,' she said, omitting the nickname she had given him in her mind. To her eternal relief, her voice didn't crack. She'd only get one chance at making a good impression, and the way his eyes narrowed made her believe that chance hung by a thin thread. 'I'm Emma Santos—the new anaesthesiologist.'

He did not move. He crossed his arms in front of his chest, the sleeves of his scrubs tightening as his muscles contracted, offering her a sight she wanted to look at longer but knew she shouldn't. Especially not with this man. She knew he had so much more to offer than just looks.

Flames licked across her skin, spreading heat throughout her body. A reaction, she rationalised, brought on from meeting this important person and not from his sexy arms. And hair. And face.

Emma cleared her throat to push those thoughts away and lifted her tablet to show it to Mark. 'In my old practice I always went through a checklist to make sure everything was in place before surgery.'

'How far down the list do you go before you

talk to the patient?' he asked, in a tone she couldn't quite identify. Not outright hostile, though she picked up on some apprehension.

This was not how she'd imagined meeting Mark Henderson would go. Instead of talking about the work they would do together, she found herself on the wrong side of unwarranted scrutiny over a surgery that didn't even involve one of his patients.

'I don't see how that is any of your concern, seeing as the patient is not on your roster.'

There was a more delicate way to handle his intrusion, Emma knew. But there was no way she would allow anyone to come into her OR questioning her when they hadn't even tried getting to know her before assuming she was terrible at her job.

'I'm the head of this department. Every patient is my patient.'

Emma flinched at the sharp barb in his voice. Her eyes drifted down to her hands and she turned the tablet around, showing Mark the list. 'Talking to the patient is actually at the very top of my list. But since I'm unfamiliar with her, and she doesn't know me either, I've examined her chart to make sure I can do what you hired me to do without disturbing her. After a formal introduction I will be able to do the proper preparation and aftercare.'

She held his stare, uncertain if she saw some remorse mixed in with his surprise, or if she just wanted him to feel that way.

His stance relaxed, his arms slowly dropping to his sides. He let out a deep breath, and with it Emma could see the tension drift away from him.

'That's good to hear. I want to make sure every patient in my ward is familiar with the entire team that is looking after them.' He paused for a moment, as if he was considering his next words. 'When Theresa told me you had arrived early, I was expecting you to be with the patient rather than already preparing the OR.'

'I thought, as a complete stranger to the patient, it would be rude to barge into her room this early in the morning.'

She met his eyes with a frown and straightened her shoulders as she prepared herself for an argument. There had been no ill intent in her actions this morning, and she had made that clear in her explanation.

The silence between them seemed to stretch out, then Mark nodded, acknowledging her words. To her surprise, a smile appeared on his lips, creating a flutter in her chest that caught her off-guard.

'The residents assigned to oncology can introduce you to all the patients. They'll be able to fill in any blanks as well. I'll see you in surgery.'

Without giving her a chance to reply, he turned around and left through the scrub room, leaving her to contemplate her first encounter with the renowned Dr Mark Henderson.

Even if Emma had tried, it couldn't have gone any worse.

If their first meeting indicated how their professional relationship would be, she could take comfort in knowing that it was only temporary.

CHAPTER TWO

THE ENCOUNTER WITH Emma had gone very differently from how Mark had expected it to earlier. He had approached the operating room expecting to have a frank conversation with her about his team and the bedside manners he expected from them. Experience had taught him that locum doctors didn't adjust well to new hospitals and held on to bad habits learned from other placements. If this was going to work, he needed to set his expectations right.

Only Emma had turned his plan on its head within the first minute of their meeting. The details on the checklist she'd shown him had contained everything he would have done himself. And instead of lecturing her about his standards of care within the oncology department, something else had happened.

Her presence in the OR had rendered him immobile for a few heartbeats, with all of his senses homing in on her as the soft scent of coconut had drifted towards him. The harsh light of the operating room hadn't affected her, and her dark, honey-toned skin had seemed to be begging to have its perceived softness verified with a brush of his fingers.

Something warm and very concerning had uncoiled itself in Mark's chest. A sensation he'd believed himself incapable of feeling. A faint ray of light piercing through the darkness of the ever-present guilt that enveloped him.

It had taken him a moment to understand what it was.

Attraction.

He'd noticed Emma as a woman of stunning beauty. Something he hadn't done since Claire had passed away, his heart too consumed with guilt. The grief had faded, and he had made peace with the fact that he would never see her again when he'd taken his wedding ring off. But the guilt remained. She'd died alone because he'd chosen to distract himself from impending pain.

The hint of desire flaring in his chest had quickly turned to anger. At himself, but also at this woman who was trespassing in his OR—and in other parts of his being—unwelcome and unbidden. So he had lashed out at her, only for her to bounce everything straight back at him.

Emma Santos did not lack determination.

Something he could appreciate despite the conflicting sensation rising within him.

Mark entered the scrub room and scrubbed his hands clean as he watched his staff getting ready to operate on Mr Norris, who was in for a tumour resection around his gallbladder. He spent extra time going over the chart and previous medical history as this was not a patient of his. Dr Andrew Fremo, one of his colleagues and Christine's husband, who had now gone on paternity leave to be with his wife, had performed the first surgery.

Mark hadn't needed to think before agreeing to take over Andrew's caseload. His own patient roster was quite full, but if extra work was what it took to ensure both his staff and patients were cared for he would take that bullet every single time.

He had broken his word once, and he worked hard to ensure it never happened again. He owed the memory of Claire that much. No matter how trivial it might seem, if he gave his word, Mark kept it.

As he stepped into the OR Mark scanned the room to see that everything was in place. The surgical nurses had set up the tray of instruments just as he liked, making him smile behind his mask. It was the little things that made the long hours worth it.

He glanced at the tablet showing the patient's chart and the surgical plan Mark had drafted earlier in the day. His eyes wandered around the present staff and locked onto Emma Santos's. Dark lashes surrounded her green eyes, creating an almost hypnotising glare.

He searched her gaze for apprehension, or any other sign of their earlier encounter. But all he found was a curious spark that spoke to him on a deeper level. His inappropriate outburst had not dampened her spirit.

'I've placed Mr Norris under anaesthesia and he's ready for you, Dr Henderson,' she said, breaking their eye contact and drawing Mark's attention back to the OR.

'Thank you, Dr Santos. All right, everyone. Let's make sure Mr Norris has the best conceivable chances at recovering. Ten blade, please.'

The second Mark set the scalpel to the patient's skin everything around him faded away. A life lay in his hands, and he reminded himself of that responsibility.

Except for his occasional request for a different instrument, the room stayed quiet as he focused on removing the tumour that grew between the gallbladder and the liver. As far as he could tell from the scans, the growth had penetrated neither of the two organs. If that was the case, they should be able to cut around the edges and remove the tumour entirely.

Only it wasn't that simple.

As Mark explored the area he could see that the walls of the gallbladder were compromised, and if he wanted to remove the whole tumour he would need to remove the organ itself. People lived a comfortable life without a gallbladder, but those people were not battling cancer on top of everything else.

Mark let out a sigh and looked up for a moment as he thought about his next steps. Emma's stare caught him off guard, and a warm sensation flared at the back of his neck. Had she been watching him the entire time? The thought broke through his focus and he caught himself looking at her. Neither of them seemed willing to break the eye contact first.

A sharp beep drew him back to reality and Emma's eyes darted to the monitor next to her. 'Blood pressure is dropping.' She rose to her feet as she said it.

Mark dropped his eyes back to the surgical field, looking for a reason for the sudden drop. He hadn't even started dissecting the tumour. There shouldn't be a rupture that led to this kind of pressure-loss.

'Where are you?' Mumbling to himself, he looked for the spontaneous bleeder. All the while he listened to Emma's voice as she kept him apprised on his vitals, helping him assess the situation as it went on.

'He's getting hypovolemic. We should hang another bag of A positive.'

Mark nodded at her suggestion, glad that she'd taken charge of her duties so he was free to focus on finding the issue at hand. 'Do it.'

He went back to work and after a few moments found a lesion on the liver and threw a suture there to stop the bleeding. Only a few more seconds and Mr Norris might have met with a different fate.

'How did this tear happen?'

Narrating his thoughts was a quirk of his in the OR, and the staff familiar with him understood he wasn't actually addressing anyone. He didn't expect an answer, so when he got one he lifted his head in surprise.

'I've seen this mentioned in a medical journal. Damage to the gallbladder can lead to weakness in the liver or liver failure, depending on the medical history of the patient. Maybe the tumour penetrating the gallbladder wall caused more strain on the liver.'

Emma was looking at him, her eyes alive with enthusiasm and something else that eluded Mark. But it was that something that vibrated inside his chest.

In one surgery she'd changed his mind about her placement in his team. If the presence of mind she had shown in the last couple of hours was an indicator of how private practice doctors trained, he would have to think twice before dismissing them the way he had before.

'Excellent call. Can you find the journal and let me know? I would like to include it in my patient notes.'

Emma nodded, the spark in her eye intensifying.

Mark had to force himself to look away. He needed to make sure Mr Norris got through this surgery with no more complications.

The skin on Emma's face tingled. The surgery had ended almost an hour ago, but adrenaline still pumped through her body and she struggled to focus on her notes. Different moments in the operating room kept replaying in her mind, and almost all of them involved Mark.

Of course they did—he was the leading surgeon on this case. Any other reason for him to stick out would be inappropriate. And Emma had had enough inappropriate work entanglements to last her the rest of her career.

Yet her heart fluttered inside her chest when she remembered those hazel eyes locking onto hers during surgery. Mark Henderson had shown her in that surgery why he was on the cover of magazines. And his stunning looks had nothing to do with it. What she had thought to be bravado turned out to be deep care and responsibility for his patients, who were going through the most challenging time of their lives. With that new understanding of him she could forgive the intensity of their first meeting, despite the memory still making her shiver with uncertainty.

Emma wanted to make the best out of her time here at Attano Memorial and learn as much as possible from the talented staff surrounding her before she started her fellowship in Rochester in two months.

As she jotted down the patient's notes she kept thinking back to the surgery, remembering all the essential details, so she could make sure they were up to the high standards Mark expected.

The standards she set for herself couldn't be any higher, so it shouldn't make a difference to how she approached them. And yet she wanted to impress him.

It was only natural, of course. He was a renowned doctor with a lot of influence. But it was more than that.

Rob was the only surgeon she'd worked with throughout her entire residency at his private practice—a move she now regretted as she witnessed her peers being so much more advanced in general medicine. It was one reason she spent so much time reading textbooks and journals in different fields. Love had made her choose poorly in her career, and she was paying the price for it.

This was Emma's chance to leave a lasting impression in the medical world. She had wasted enough time on things that brought her only pain. Her fellowship would be the last leg of her medical training and then she would have achieved everything she'd set out to do.

Once she got to her goal she would have to find the courage to get tested. But it could wait. At least that was what she told herself. Gardner Syndrome usually showed itself in adolescence. Emma had reached her early thirties without a single sign of a tumour.

She still needed to know, but there was no way she would let herself get distracted from her medical training again. One failed romance had already taken enough time from her studies.

Engrossed in her own thoughts, she didn't notice someone approaching. The chair they pulled out scraped over the floor, creating a loud sound that tore Emma's attention back to reality.

As if her thoughts had made him manifest in front of her, Mark turned the chair around and straddled it. He crossed his arms on top of the backrest and looked at her with those warm brown eyes that sent a searing spark through her. He folded his arms in front of him and rested his chin on top of them.

Emma became instantly aware of his proximity. Her eyes glided over him, taking in the enticing view. How did he have the time to stay in that kind of shape?

'Are you checking me out?' he asked in a low baritone voice, making her flinch at his bluntness.

As if she would ever go there with a superior of hers. Again.

'Of course not!' she said, cringing at how she came across as if she had very much been checking him out. Which she had. 'How can I help you, Dr Henderson?'

'Excellent work on Mr Norris' surgery. Theresa told me you transferred here from San Francisco. What made you come here?'

You. Though Emma couldn't tell him that. Especially not now.

At one point she'd believed he might be the one to cure her from the disease she might carry dormant within her. She had watched the oncologists follow his regime of pain management for her mother, easing her last days. Despite how hard it had been to watch, it had inspired Emma.

She'd wanted to be a doctor who could help just the way her mother's doctors had.

When the opportunity to work at the same hospital as him had come up, she'd said yes with almost no hesitation. And it hadn't come a moment too soon. After spending her residency years putting people to sleep for elective plastic surgery, she'd yearned for a change. Emma wanted to be challenged, and to add her own knowledge to the growing field of medicine.

And more recently there had been a quiet voice in the back of her mind, urging her not to settle for less than she wanted. What if her mother had passed her condition on to her? If she wasn't able to be a doctor any more, what would her legacy look like?

'I completed my residency, so my time in San Francisco was up, and I needed to move on.'

As Emma didn't want to tell him the truth, she went with a simplified version. She would never tell him how her manipulative ex-boyfriend had tried to force her to pass up the opportunity of a lifetime, because it didn't suit his own needs.

'I had a gap between completing my board exam and my fellowship position, so I came here.'

Mark shifted his head to the side, his eyes

never leaving her as he contemplated her words. 'So, you're not from California.'

A statement, Emma observed, and her gaze shifted from him to the tablet in front of her. His eyes made her acutely aware of his presence, along with the faint scent of pine drifting from him. Even after a four-hour surgery, he still looked and smelled fresh. She felt as if she needed a shower before continuing this conversation.

The images of Mark and a shower combined themselves in her head, making the heat rise from her stomach to her cheeks.

'No, I'm not. I came to the States to study. My family still lives in Brazil. Is my accent still that bad after all the years I've spent here?'

'It's not bad, at all. I like it. There is a certain melody to the way you speak.'

A smirk appeared at the corners of his lips, and she wondered if he had noticed the tinge of rose on her face.

'It's rather unusual for an anaesthesiologist to do their residency in a private practice. Why did you choose that path?'

His eyes bored into her, and Emma almost squirmed under the probing look. He was asking about the dark corners of her mind, where she didn't want anyone to look. How could she tell a man like Mark that she had chosen to damage her career prospects because of love? Because she had been blind enough to fall for the fake promises of a man who was only looking out for himself?

'It seemed like a good choice at the time.'

She didn't trust herself to say anything else. The last thing she wanted was this man she admired judging her for the mistake she regretted most in her life.

He nodded, seeming content with her answer. 'What field are you specialising in for your fellowship?'

'Emergency medicine,' she replied with a sigh of relief, and saw a spark of curiosity ignite in his eyes.

'That's an interesting offshoot from anaesthesiology. Where are you headed?'

Despite anticipating the question, Emma's stomach still did a small turn, and she bit her lip, felt the blush in her cheeks intensifying.

'Rochester,' she said.

Mark's lips parted in surprise. 'You're joining the programme at Whitebridge?'

Emma nodded. An odd mix of pride and embarrassment overcame her every time she told someone about her fellowship. It was a competitive programme, and she was one of the few selected to work and learn at one of the most prestigious hospitals in the country.

The Whitebridge Institute was also the place where Mark had studied and worked for most of his career.

'It hasn't quite sunk in yet, even though I'm starting in a couple of weeks.'

'Not a lot of people get invited to that programme.'

His voice had adopted a strange quality Emma couldn't place. He sounded almost apprehensive. It made her heart stutter in her chest. Did he not have fond feelings about his time in Rochester? Was there something she didn't know about the institute?

'How long have you lived in the States? It must be a few years at this point,' he said, ripping her out of her contemplations.

'I haven't really left since med school. I was lucky to get a scholarship, or I might not have been able to study here.'

Her mother had received her diagnosis after Emma had left the country to study. Otherwise she might have never left Brazil, not wanting to put so much distance between her and her ailing parent.

'Luck is not usually a deciding factor in scholarships,' he said with a hint of humour.

She caught her breath. But she must have misread his tone—because there was no way Mark

Henderson would flirt with her. What else could give his voice such a playful ring?

'Maybe the panel liked the melody accompanying my words,' she said with a laugh, as she tried to deflect the heat his probing gaze drew to the surface of her skin.

'There is a lot to like at first glance.'

Emma opened her lips to reply, but the words died in her throat. There it was again. A light vibration beneath his words that caused a warm spark to bounce down her spine, settling right behind her navel. This could not be happening. There was no reality in which it was acceptable for her to be flirting with her boss. Ever.

'I should go prepare for my next surgery,' she said, in an attempt to overcome the odd sensations battling inside her.

As she got up, Mark reached out and placed a hand on her forearm, halting her. The warmth prickling in her cheeks cascaded into a wave that swept through her body, leaving a hot sensation where he had touched her.

'I meant what I said about surgery. It's a tough specialty we're in, so while your quick thinking won't save a lot of lives, it will give our patients an edge. And in their situation they need every advantage that we can give them.' He paused and looked at her with an intense expression. Then he lifted his hand to let her go.

'If you are serious about your work here, then I welcome you to the team and I look forward to teaching you.'

Emma's stomach tied itself into a knot, and she swallowed to ease away the lump in her throat so she could answer him with composure. 'Thank you, Dr Henderson.'

'Please, call me Mark.'

'I will see you in our next surgery, Mark.'

His name had dropped so fast off her lips that she almost repeated it, just to hear it again.

CHAPTER THREE

MARK SAT BEHIND the desk in his office, sipping his coffee and looking through his patient files for the day. There was only one patient on his surgical schedule: Georgina Williams.

The last week had been interesting in many ways, with Emma Santos being at the centre of his contemplations. She had integrated herself into his team, and his attending surgeons were already gushing about her competency and hard-working attitude.

What he hadn't expected was the effect she had on him after just one week of working together. He treated all his staff with the same amount of attention and respect. A pleasant working environment where everyone could work well and be honest with each other was a point of pride for him. But something beyond that drove him to seek Emma out. The warm tendrils of attraction he felt drew him in each time he let his guard down.

It was a feeling Mark could not reconcile within himself. The flutter he was experiencing in his chest, the heat igniting the blood in his veins whenever he let his thoughts stray towards her—those were things for available people. He was the furthest he could be from that.

He'd never even entertained the thought of another woman. When Claire had needed him the most, he had failed to be a proper husband to her. Though it pained him, Mark had admitted to himself a long time ago that he wasn't strong enough for what life had thrown at him. All he had left to do now was to be the best kind of doctor he could be. That was where his strength lay.

Downing the last bit of coffee from his mug, Mark got up. He grabbed the tablet off his desk and made his way to Georgina's room for the pre-op check before her surgery in the afternoon. He'd opened up her patient chart on the tablet in his hand and was scrolling through the pages, looking for her latest lab results, when he noticed the file was being edited.

With furrowed brows, he watched as notes appeared, giving him all the information he needed and doing all the pre-op checks he'd planned on doing himself. His residents knew he liked to do it himself.

But the notes he was looking at right now

were almost exactly how he'd make them. Could it be Emma?

Mark cleared his throat as an unexpected dryness spread through his mouth. And as he entered the patient's room, his suspicion was confirmed.

Emma stood next to the patient's bed, talking to Georgina and updating the chart. Between the chatter and the noises from the monitor connected to her, neither of them had heard his knock or him entering the room.

Emma stood tall in her heels—much taller than he remembered from their surgeries in the past week. Her white lab coat covered most of her body, but underneath she wore a deep blue woollen dress with a dipping neckline that left just enough to the imagination. Her dark curls flowed over her shoulders in tantalising waves.

Diligent and beautiful. A combination that would force many men to their knees.

Not him, though.

The tempting sense of attraction that stirred in his chest when he looked at her consumed his mind whenever he let his thoughts drift. The warmth emanating from her sought him out, finding the cracks in his armour and awakening a dormant part of him. But it only took a second for that feeling to be gripped by the guilt living in his heart. How could he look at another woman and feel the faint whisper of desire?

Unnoticed, he looked from Georgina to Emma and then his eyes landed on Harald, Georgina's husband, who sat on a chair and shrugged with a small smile as the two women shared a laugh.

Mark remembered a time when he had been the spouse sitting in one of these chairs, trying his best to project an aura of confidence. As a husband, your role was to support your sick wife. You needed to be strong, so your partner could lean on them.

The toll of that had been greater than Mark had expected. Until Claire's diagnosis he had only ever experienced the disease from a physician's point of view. A viewpoint he'd slipped into when her condition had got worse. As a doctor, he could get away with being emotionally distant. Only she hadn't needed another doctor. She had needed her husband.

Emma's laughter pulled him out of his contemplation of past regrets and Mark swallowed the lump building in his throat as his gaze drifted over her once more. No one ever looked good under the fluorescent lights of a hospital room. But somehow all Mark could focus on was her wavy dark brown hair and how it would feel if he ran his fingers through it. Silky, smooth, smelling of coconut and filling his head with fantasies…

As he stepped forward Georgina spotted him first, before Emma turned around to face him, a small smile on her lips. 'Perfect timing! Mrs Williams has just asked about the upcoming procedure. Do you have time to walk her through it step by step?'

'Please call me Georgina. I figure someone who wants to know so much about me gets to call me by my first name.' Georgina waved her hand at Emma, who chuckled again.

'She still makes me call her Mrs Williams, mind you,' her husband said from his seat, turning her chuckle into a full laugh.

'I see you're in great spirits today,' said Mark. 'Good. Keeping a positive attitude is important for a quick recovery.'

Mark made another step forward, positioning himself next to Emma. His shoulder brushed hers when he passed her, sending a spark down his arm. He tried his best to ignore the sensation while focusing on his patient.

'I'm sure Dr Santos has already introduced herself. She's joining us for a couple of weeks as our staff anaesthesiologist. I want to give her as many opportunities as possible to hone her skills while she's here with us. So I'm going to ask her to present your case, Georgina. If there is anything unclear just let me know and we will go back a step.'

Emma's lips parted as Mark nodded at her, clearly expecting her to walk Georgina through all the steps of her surgery. Even though she wasn't a surgeon, and hadn't received any surgical training, she had studied the procedure for her own preparations. So she caught herself and cleared her throat, looking at the tablet in her hands to find the notes she'd made last night.

'Georgina Williams, age thirty-two, diagnosed with a tumour on her left ovary. Scheduled for an oophorectomy this afternoon...' She presented the patient's history to Mark, who nodded at her with a hint of a smile before turning back to Georgina.

'What that means is that this afternoon we will remove your left ovary to get the potentially malignant tissue at its origin. We'll send some samples to the lab to confirm whether it's malignant.'

Emma focused her attention on their patient, and it helped her banish the tingling heat that spread through her stomach. From the notes in the chart, Emma could tell that the tumour had been discovered quite recently. But despite that

Georgina always smiled and didn't seem to fear her diagnosis.

It was a quality Emma envied. She wanted to be just as brave with her own diagnosis, but she couldn't even talk herself into having a test. Only two more years and then her training would be done. She would worry about her next steps then.

Mark stepped up to her, drawing her attention. All her senses homed in on him as she registered his proximity to her. This was a more immediate concern she needed to deal with. The pangs of heat cascading through her body whenever she was close to him were inappropriate for more reasons that she could count.

'Why are we performing a partial oophorectomy rather than a full hysterectomy?' He looked at her as he asked the question.

'The scans suggest the tumour is isolated in one ovary. To preserve the patient's reproductive organs, an oophorectomy is less invasive.'

Emma hadn't expected to be questioned the same way interns were, but it made sense. He had told her he looked forward to teaching her.

Mark nodded with a smile that caused a wave of warm sparks to ignite behind her navel.

'After the surgery, Georgina, you will need to recover from the stress we'll be putting your body under before we transfer you to an oncologist if you need chemotherapy.'

Emma continued her explanation and saw a spark of fear enter Georgina's eyes—a look she was familiar with. Emma's chest tightened.

She stepped closer to her and rested her hand on hers, giving it a reassuring squeeze. 'I know it sounds scary, but if you do need chemotherapy I'm familiar with some remedies for a few of the side effects. Make sure a nurse pages me, and I can tell you what helped in my case.'

Georgina raised her eyebrows.

It was only then Emma realised what she had said. 'Oh, no, not me. My mother had cancer.'

Georgina breathed out a sigh of relief and Emma took a step back, daring to look at Mark again. Any composure she had built up melted away in an instant as she saw the warm glow of sympathy in his eyes. He'd clearly caught the piece of personal information she'd revealed by accident.

'We also have you scheduled for a visit from the gynaecologist to harvest some of your eggs, if necessary, as well as talk to you about any questions on fertility that you might have,' Mark said, looking at both Harald and Georgina as he spoke. 'If you need chemotherapy it will impact your healthy eggs, which is why we like to harvest them before you move on with your treatment. Ideally, we'll also fertilise the eggs before we freeze them, but that's something the two of you can discuss with Dr Clark when she comes to see you.'

Emma's heart went out to the couple. Georgina's tumour had thrown all their plans into disarray—to the point where they now had to discuss their future children on a clinical level.

It was a concern that crept into her own mind every now and again. While Emma didn't have any siblings, she'd grown up on the same street as her cousins, so she hadn't lacked friends her own age to bond with. Whenever she'd got into fights with her parents she'd found shelter in her cousin Livia's room, where they would contemplate the hardship of being a teenager in the Santos clan.

Even now her big family was a source of comfort, even though they lived on a different continent. She couldn't imagine her life any other way, and yearned to have her own family one day. Though if she did have Gardner's how she made that family would differ from how she'd imagined.

It was another reason to get an answer to that open question. And one more reason she didn't want to know. How was she supposed to make all these decisions on her own?

Emma cleared her throat, forcing those intrusive thoughts away. She needed to focus on the task ahead of her. 'And I think that is the gist of it. Are there any questions left on your side?'

Georgina looked at her husband for a moment before shaking her head, and that slight gesture caused Emma's heart to twinge in her chest. That was what she wanted. A person to help her through the tough times she might be facing. Someone who understood what she needed with a mere look.

In a different life, she'd thought Rob to be that person for her. She'd been too wrapped up in his manipulations and her own insecurities to see their relationship for what it had been— nothing more than a means to further his private practice at the cost of her career.

'No, all good here. Let's kick this tumour's butt.'

Harald laughed at his wife's choice of words.

'Good. Keep your spirits up, and we'll see you this afternoon.'

Mark smiled at Georgina before turning around and nodded at Harald on his way out. He paused at the door, holding it open for Emma. They walked to the nurses' station, where they both deposited their tablets. The hair on her nape rose as his brown eyes met hers.

A week had passed since she'd arrived in Chicago, and the very thing she'd sworn wouldn't happen was happening. In front of her eyes, her respect for Mark and his work had been transformed into a subtle pull of attraction. Whenever she let her mind wander she ended up thinking about him.

They'd recovered their relationship after a rocky start, and were making an excellent team inside the OR. More than once she'd thought she had seen his gaze wander over to her. Had he been checking her out or judging her work? The thought that he might look at her as a woman almost made her laugh in derision. He was Mark Henderson, award-winning surgeon and researcher. He was her boss. She was just a doctor from the poorer part of Brazil, who couldn't even take a simple test to save her life.

'It's good to see her so enthusiastic about her treatment,' Emma said, and Mark nodded.

He leaned his hip against the counter of the nurses' station as he turned to face her, his arms crossed in front of his chest, enticing her to let her gaze roam for a bit.

'It's a rare sight to see such an upbeat patient. A good sign for the course of her potential treatment. Patients with a positive outlook have a much higher rate of recovery.'

'I imagine it's not always easy to inspire that kind of mood.'

Mark's hands dropped to his sides at that

comment, his eyes drifting away for a moment. 'No, not really. Most people in our care are looking at a worse battle. We get a lot of patients from out of state, looking at us for their third and fourth opinions.'

He said it so casually, as if it had never occurred to him what it meant that people sought him out when they had no other hope left.

'They want to be treated by the best. They want you. I can understand that,' she said.

His dark eyes came back to her, a strange expression fluttering over his face. He seemed confused. But there was no way he didn't know why people were travelling here to be treated by his team of doctors. Or was he just not used to hearing it in such plain words?

Her train of thought came to an abrupt stop when his lips parted in a smile, sending her heart slamming against her chest.

A faint blush sneaked onto Emma's cheeks, making Mark wonder what thoughts were rattling around in her head that were intrusive enough to make her flush all on her own. He didn't want to admit how much he enjoyed watching it happen. Was she thinking of him? Or was he projecting his own inner turmoil back at her?

Despite his desire to keep things professional,

he wanted to learn more about her. The compassion she'd shown Georgina was the energy he wanted in the oncology department. The road to recovery for all patients was a difficult one, and Emma would soon learn that they didn't earn as many victories as they wanted.

Before Claire had got sick herself, they had both poured a lot of their professional lives into researching cancer and developing new treatments. She'd focused on different ways of relieving pain while he looked for overall treatment options. It was Claire who had made a connection between the different patients they'd observed and their overall personalities. She had got sick before she could finish her research paper on it, but he remembered how much of it she'd applied to herself. No matter how tired the radiation therapy had made her feel, she had tried to smile—for herself as much as for him.

Knowing that Emma had a loved one suffering from cancer explained a lot about her compassion. It added another layer to her, making her more than she seemed. She intrigued Mark—something that was even worse than the attraction he felt stirring in his chest. Curiosity wasn't something he could indulge with his colleagues. Emma was here to learn from him, not to be a target of his misguided attraction.

'Is your mother a cancer survivor?' he asked, to distract himself from his thoughts.

Regret turned his stomach as profound pain contorted her face.

'No, unfortunately not' was all she said, her eyes dropping so he couldn't see her full face any more.

The expression his question had summoned to her face was one he was familiar with himself. For a split second the urge to confide his own loss to her grew inside his chest. He had put her in a situation where she'd had to reveal her past pain to him. What surprised him was how much he wanted to share his with her.

Most of his days Mark spent shrouded in the oppressive darkness that was the memory of his final days with Claire. Despite the guilt of missing her last moments still clinging to his heart, he had transformed his feelings into something to serve him. A drive to hold himself and his staff to the highest standards possible, so that no spouse would have to feel the same way he did. So that no one would need to bear the weight of everything all by themselves, like Harald was doing for his wife right now. As Mark had failed to do for Claire.

That kind of drive was another thing that he and Emma had in common. The woman was getting more intriguing by the minute, and he felt his surrounding darkness ease as he got to know her better. It was an odd sensation, that was unbidden but not unpleasant. He wanted to know more about her, despite knowing that it was best if he didn't. Attachment to anyone was something he tried to avoid.

'Have you seen anything of Chicago yet?' he asked, to distract himself from the urge to reveal his darker thoughts to her.

'No, I only arrived the night before yesterday.' She pressed her lips together before chuckling. 'No rest for the wicked.'

'I'll show you when we have a day off together. You shouldn't leave for Rochester before you've eaten rib tips from one of the barbecue stalls at the waterfront.'

'Rib tips? I thought you Chicagoans were all about your deep-dish pizza?'

Her lips parted in a smile, and the urge to reach out to feel her skin underneath his fingertips resurfaced.

'We can eat deep-dish pizza, but you would be missing out. Don't let the clever marketing of the pizza industry deceive you. Trust me, you will thank me later.'

His quip drew another laugh from her lips, a sound vibrating through his body and igniting a gentle heat across his skin.

Why had he invited her out? He hadn't had

time to contemplate his suggestion before his mouth had formed the words, uttering an invitation he hadn't meant to extend. The tension arching through his body should be something he buried and ignored. Not acted on by inviting her out on a date.

No, it was a professional courtesy—not a date. Emma would head to the Whitebridge Institute after her short stint here, and Mark knew that the chief of surgery would want him to make her experience a good one. He wanted her to leave thinking of all the great things she had learned at Attano Memorial.

'One of the surgical residents is running pre-op procedures today. So I will see you in the OR,' he said, his mouth a thin line as he gave her only a curt nod before leaving.

Mark needed to watch himself. To enjoy the warmth coming from Emma was one thing. Another thing was to act on it.

Taking a deep breath, he forced himself to walk away and to focus on the fact that they made an excellent team. In surgery, as well as when she was walking a patient through each step of their upcoming procedure, Emma showed him the depth of her compassion and skill. Their interactions with each other were flowing and seamless, even without them having worked together before.

This kind of quality was much more significant in Mark's world than something as fleeting as attraction.

Georgina's surgery would be the first test for that.

CHAPTER FOUR

EMMA GRABBED HER phone out of the pocket of her lab coat to check the time. Her conversation with Mark had gone on much longer than she'd thought it had. They would be in surgery two hours from now. With all the pre-op check-ups done, she didn't need to do much more to prepare for the procedure. Only her pre-surgery checklist remained, and Emma needed to be in the operating room for that.

As she walked down the corridor she caught a glimpse of herself. Having worked at a private clinic, Emma had got used to dressing up every morning, only changing into scrubs when it was time for surgery. Rob had insisted that the patients only saw her in nice clothes, wanting to sell them an experience on top of their procedure. He'd criticised her on several occasions for looking too casual, and asked her to change before leaving the house.

In the corridors of Attano Memorial, it surprised her to see no one in anything else other than scrubs or a lab coat. She even saw some of the staff arriving in scrubs in the car park.

Painful humiliation stabbed Emma in the chest as she looked down on herself again. She had left, regained control of her own life, and yet she still hung on to the habits she'd cultivated to please Rob. Not only had she lost out on the level of training an anaesthetist would have received in a hospital environment, she'd also forgotten how to be comfortable in her own skin.

With her family being so far away, the people she worked with were the closest thing she had to a support system here in the States. As a doctor, she didn't exactly have oodles of free time, so the only people she could rely on were her co-workers. Emma wanted to blend in with her new colleagues—wanted to belong and feel comfortable.

Not too comfortable, though. With the friendliness of the staff surrounding her, it was way too easy to forget that this was only a temporary assignment and that before long she would pack her car again and be on her way to Rochester.

Her first on-call shift started today—a prospect that made her insides lurch with both excitement and dread alike. During her day shifts at the hospital, they always assigned her to the

oncology department, working on cases with
the surgeons there. That changed for the on-call
shifts. To ensure the strain on the anaesthetist
was as minimal as possible, the chief of surgery
there had put them all into one large rotation,
so that each of them only had to work one on-
call shift every couple of weeks.

This would be her only on-call shift in her
time at Attano Memorial. A prospect that
wouldn't seem as daunting if she had worked in
such an environment before. But thanks to Rob,
and his web of lies, Emma's unpreparedness
stood out like a sore thumb. Which, at the end of
the day, she had only herself to blame for. While
she had been tricked and lied to, each decision
she'd made had been her own. The knowledge
of how willingly blind she had been stung as
much as the lies he had enveloped her in.

She tried not to be too hard on herself, but
it was difficult. Back in Brazil she would have
had her cousins to advise her. They butted into
her affairs more often than she wanted, giving
her guidance without her asking for it. It was
something that had annoyed her back then. Now
she missed them. They would have warned her
about Rob even if she hadn't wanted to hear it.
But being all alone, in a place that had felt very
different from Brazil, Emma had leaned on the

person who had extended to her some comfort. Even if he had done so for his own goals.

Looking back at their relationship now filled Emma with a sense of horror and sadness beyond words. She couldn't grasp how much she had let herself tolerate when the writing had been on the wall all the time. But instead of seeing him for what he was, she'd kept finding ways to make excuses for him, giving him the benefit of the doubt over and over again. She had tried to discuss her mother's death with him, and to tell him about what she might be carrying within her. She had tried to turn to him for support, to see if together they might find out the truth.

Rob had told her their surgical schedule was too busy and that he wasn't sure they could afford to take time off at a pivotal moment for his practice. Maybe later, he had suggested. After that, she had felt too self-conscious and exposed to bring it up again, thinking she was selfish to want him to take so much time away from his work.

With a sigh, Emma pushed those thoughts away and opened the door of her locker in the residents' changing room, taking the stethoscope from around her neck and hanging it on the open door before removing her lab coat. She grabbed the folded scrubs from inside and paused when she spotted the object lying beneath them: an old Polaroid picture of her with her parents, on the day she'd got accepted into med school.

The photo had travelled with her wherever she went, as a reminder to keep going. Her mother had been so proud when she'd got the acceptance letter that she had planned a *churrasco* for the same evening, inviting the entire street to celebrate the fact that her daughter was going to be a doctor.

It was the last time she remembered seeing her mother full of life. The next time she'd made it back home during a break at medical school was the time when she had been confronted with her mother's diagnosis and rapidly deteriorating health.

She had flown back to Brazil to see her mother as much as she could, but a visit during her second year had turned out to be the last one. The pain of her mother's death had been so raw and all-consuming that she hadn't wanted to go back to med school. Her father had had to physically remove her from his house to get her to go back to the States.

The memory now made her smile to herself, but back then tears had stained her cheeks.

The possibility that she might suffer from the same disease her mother had died of infused her with a naked fear that took possession of her entire body when she thought about it. But the terror demanded space she couldn't afford at the moment. She had to make up for time lost. Her peers were all ahead of her in clinical hours and research, so getting back on track was Emma's key priority.

This also meant that she avoided talking about her mother in front of anyone, as it invited more questions than she wanted. Until she'd found herself in that room with Mark and their patient and the words had tumbled out of her mouth. Without trying, he had slipped past her defences and uncovered a piece of information she didn't usually volunteer to anyone.

What had made Emma's breath hitch in her throat had been the warm glow of sympathy in his eyes when he'd learned of her mother's death. He'd seemed to understand her pain without needing to ask any more questions than the one he had. Had he spent enough time surrounded by cancer patients that he felt their pain as if it was his own? Or had he, too, lost someone dear to him to cancer?

Either way, she had glimpsed the kind soul that lay behind the unyielding and devastatingly handsome exterior.

No, she couldn't think about Mark in such terms, Emma reminded herself, pulling the scrub top over her head and slipping into the trousers. Kind, smart, talented. Those were acceptable words with which to describe her boss. Handsome? No, not allowed.

Her interest in him was professional, and she couldn't afford to miss this opportunity to work with him because she found herself distracted by his alluring eyes. Or his handsome face. Or the fine lines of muscle she'd spotted beneath the loose fabric of his shirt. If she could only run her hand over one of those lines…maybe that would be enough to satisfy her curiosity.

A hot sensation licked over her cheeks and Emma caught her breath. *Absolutely no more daydreaming*, she told herself. That path only led to more heartbreak, and she shouldn't even be contemplating anything like that. What made her think a successful surgeon like Mark would be interested in her, anyway?

With a sigh, she raked her fingers through her hair, pulling it into a tight bun that sat at her nape. She had surgery preparations to make. Rather than focus on Dr Handsome, and the scrubs that revealed as much as they obscured, she vowed to concentrate on their work as a team and what she could learn in the precious few weeks that they had. He'd let her present Georgina's case, and that showed her he was keen on teaching her. They were an excellent team—in the strictest of professional senses.

She straightened herself as she wrapped the stethoscope around her neck again and left for the operating room.

Done with her pre-op checklist, and having checked all items off, Emma retreated into the scrub room to re-scrub. As she washed her hands, the doors on the far side of the operating room opened. Two interns pushed Georgina in, with Mark walking next to her. The surgery was not due to begin for another thirty minutes, so they were a bit early.

Emma peered through the window into the OR, her eyes fixated on Mark. Despite her standing at the lit window he didn't see her, his full attention on his patient. His hand grasped Georgina's as they shared a laugh, which made his entire face light up. The fine lines around his eyes told a story of many smiles, and Emma wanted to reach through the glass to touch them, to feel the captivating curve of his lips under her fingertips.

The flutter originating in her stomach radiated through her body, and to drive those intrusive thoughts away Emma splashed some of the cold water on her face. What had happened to no daydreaming about the boss? If she lost focus that fast, she'd never get through a whole surgery with him in such close proximity.

The soft expression on his face as he spoke to their patient betrayed the stern nature he projected when talking to his staff. Emma glimpsed a profound vulnerability hiding beneath the gruff exterior, and for a moment an uncomfortable pinch settled in her chest. He and his patient were having a personal moment that she shouldn't be watching. But Georgina needed to be started on her first round of medication in a couple of minutes, so she would be ready for surgery.

Emma dried her hands with a fresh towel and took a face mask, tying it behind her head and pressing the button to open the door. It slid open without a sound and she walked in, freezing in her step when the conversation between Mark and Georgina didn't stop. It seemed neither of them was aware of her.

'Of course. The second we finish here I will update your husband on the surgery.' Mark smiled at Georgina and took her hand when she reached out to him.

'Thank you, Dr Henderson. You know, Dr Fremo warned me about your charm, but he forgot to mention the good looks. I should have put on my nice hospital gown for you,' she said, drawing a soft chuckle from his lips that mingled with her laugh.

'Georgina, I enjoy being your doctor, so don't let my wife hear any of this or I won't be your doctor for long.'

'Oh, you and Dr Santos are married and you work together every day? I don't know if I could be around Harry all day.'

Mark laughed again, shaking his head. 'No, Dr Santos is not my wife. How did you get that idea?'

'I'm a matchmaker by trade. I know desire when I see it.' Georgina smiled, looking at him with a spark in her eyes.

'We make a good team. I think that is what you may have glimpsed.'

Emma stood still in the doorframe, wishing she had made them aware of her earlier. In her mind, the noise of the door should have been enough, but she realised now that they hadn't heard her enter, and she'd intruded in a very private conversation. She didn't know how to move now without seeming as if she had been eavesdropping. An impression she wanted to avoid.

One of the OR nurses came to her rescue, opening the door on the far side of the operating room to wheel in a monitor. The surrounding commotion ended their conversation and allowed Emma to step up to her spot. She glanced at Mark as he stood up, hoping the mask obscured her expression enough so that he wouldn't notice she had heard everything he'd said to Georgina.

Her mind was still processing what she had overheard. He was married.

Emma's chest tightened, and a stabbing pain left her paralysed for a few breaths. Why did she care? Mark had been off-limits before she had even met him. Finding out that he was married just cemented her 'absolutely no daydreaming of any kind' rule.

'All right, Georgina. This medication will make you sleepy.'

She got up from her chair and headed over to the instrument tray, popping the syringe out of the vacuum-sealed packaging and double-checking the numbers on her tablet before filling the needle with the medication and injecting it through a small port in the crook of the patient's arm.

'Will you count down from ten for me?'

She tried to smile at Georgina, to reassure her, thankful that the mask hid most of her face as the woman started counting down. Her voice trailed off when she got to eight, and the number seven didn't make it past her lips.

The OR around her burst into life as everyone prepared to start the surgery. Emma picked

up the curved laryngoscope from her tray of instruments, intubating Georgina and connecting
the valve of the tube to the aspirator.

'We're good to start, Dr Henderson,' Emma
said, and it took more effort than she'd thought
it would to keep her voice from cracking. Her
mind was racing.

Biting back a sigh, Emma settled down on her
chair and took a few deep breaths. Right now
she had a job to do. And at least she now knew
that the attraction she'd sensed was not mutual.

The entire team in the OR had followed the surgical plan without a single hitch, leaving Mark
pleased as they wheeled the still unconscious
Georgina out and back to her room, where her
husband would be waiting.

He'd caught himself looking over to Emma
from time to time, seen her dark eyes narrowed
and fixated on the monitor sitting next to her.
She had been quiet throughout the procedure
and hadn't shown any interest when he'd started
walking the interns through the steps of the oophorectomy as he performed the surgery. He'd
sensed something was off, and the urge to in-
vestigate had grown stronger as the surgery had
gone on.

As the nurses transported Georgina back to
her room, Mark turned to the interns. 'Grab the

sample that we biopsied and bring it down to the lab. Once we have the results you can update Mrs Williams' chart and page me so we can review it together.'

Mark turned around, wanting to catch Emma before she left, but her assigned seat was already empty. He had not turned his back for more than five minutes. She must have left in a hurry.

'Did you see Emma leave?' he asked Theresa, who was preparing the room for the next surgery.

'Emma?' She raised an eyebrow at him. 'Dr Santos left a few seconds ago. She's probably finishing her notes on the surgery somewhere.'

Mark nodded and went on pursuit. Something wasn't right, and he wanted to understand it straight away.

He poked his head through the door of the break room, but she wasn't there. She wasn't at the nurses' station either, and when he asked the nurse there about her, she indicated that she had seen her come by just a couple of minutes ago.

His options running low, Mark started checking the on-call rooms, and found her in the second one he checked on his floor.

He would have searched every single room in the hospital just to find her.

That thought lingered at the edge of his mind—something he couldn't admit to himself. Would he have done it for anyone else, or would he have just let them cool off and then catch up with them the following day?

'I was looking for you,' he said as he spotted Emma sitting on the top bunk with her tablet on her lap.

Her eyes narrowed as she looked at him, sending an icy shiver down his spine. Now he was sure there was something not right between them.

'You found me. How can I help you?'

'You left so fast after the surgery. I just wanted to check in on you.'

He stepped closer to the bunk she sat on, her elevated position putting them at the same height. The dark waves of hair were contained in a tight knot, which granted him a view of her neck and shoulders, and for a moment he wondered how her skin would feel underneath his fingers. Would she be as soft as she looked?

'I did my part and I didn't need to stick around. I administered the drug to take her out of anaesthesia, so now I only need to check in on her after she's woken up to see how to manage her pain.'

Why was he chasing after her? While he would admit that he liked his doctors to work in harmony with one another, he knew disagreements happened to the best of them. That someone should choose to step away so as to not escalate conflict was a good thing. Instead of pressing her, Mark should take her words at face value and leave. It would be the professional thing to do.

After all, what other reason did he have for his presence here?

He didn't have any interest in Emma that went beyond their working relationship, so he should say nothing more and leave.

'Did I do something I'm not aware of?' The words left his lips before he could stop them.

Emma released a breath. 'No, I came here to write up my notes before getting some rest. I'm working an on-call shift today.'

Her words were short. He sensed there was something she wasn't telling him. A strange need inside him pushed him to probe further. He felt an almost irresistible draw from her. His hand seemed to demand he reach out to smooth the frown from her lips with a gentle touch. To untangle her hair so he could find out how her locks felt between his fingers.

Control almost slipped from his grasp and Mark took a step back, aware of every inch of air between them. As much as his insides protested, he needed to let go of this conversation and move on.

'I find the bed over there the most comfortable. It's close to the door, so people avoid it,' he said to change the subject. He pointed at the bed opposite. 'Trust me. You'll sleep better.'

Emma eyed him for a moment, and he could tell she was weighing her words. In the end she gave him a faint smile, and Mark caught his breath at the sight. It was like a sunrise after a frosty night, dispersing the dark fog gathered around him.

'Thanks for the tip. I'll try it out.' As she braced herself to jump off the top bunk the seam of her scrub top caught the metal rod of the bedpost, causing her to lose her footing.

Mark reacted instantly, closing the gap between them with one step and wrapping his arms around her waist to prevent her from falling to the ground. Her eyes widened in surprise, and she looked at him as a gasp escaped her lips. He met her gaze, felt her scent filling his nose and clouding his thoughts, enticing him to close the last few inches between them and steal a taste of her lips. He just needed to lean in a bit…

'Mark, I…'

Her breath fluttered, grazing his cheeks, and her eyes narrowed. She relaxed against his arms, giving in to his pull—and then the shrill alarm of her beeper cut through the moment between them.

Despite his better judgement, he hesitated to let go of her. He was enjoying the closeness a lot more than he should.

'There's a trauma case incoming. I have to go,' Emma said as she looked at the pager.

For a moment their eyes locked again. The moment they'd almost shared was reflected in her expression. Grabbing her tablet from the top bunk, she squeezed by him and left without another word.

Mark sat down on the lower bunk behind him, burying his face in his hands. How had he let it get so far, so fast?

Emma had something incredible about her that he struggled to put into words. Whenever he was around her the clouds around him lifted, making way for the warm light emanating from her. By her side, the pain of his past seemed less. But could he let himself feel attracted to someone when the guilt of Claire's death still clung to his heart?

Memory came rushing back into his consciousness. This entire time he hadn't thought of her, and the realisation thundered through his body. His draw towards Emma had made him forget everything except for the fire a mere glance of her ignited beneath his skin.

Mark had thought he'd moved on when he'd taken off his wedding ring. Yet now, confronted with his obvious attraction to Emma, he couldn't help but feel the weight of his past mistakes with Claire. She served as his beacon, as well as a warning. Her memory drove him to be a better doctor, but he doubted he could be a better man.

The fact that he could still feel this kind of attraction was a new discovery. He didn't know what to think of it. Or what to do. One thing was certain: Mark could not act on the desire uncoiling itself inside his chest.

The noise of his own beeper interrupted his thoughts and he jerked up, looking at the message appearing on the screen.

911 in OR Two

He forced himself to push all thoughts of Emma aside. His obligation to his patients would always come first.

Her heart pounded against her chest with such urgency that Emma thought if she opened her mouth it would leap right out of her body. The nurse preparing the operating room had informed her they were expecting the victim of a car crash. Her first case on her on-call shift.

Emma took a few deep breaths, calming the turmoil in her chest. Images of Mark flashed through her head, his lips so close to hers she had almost been able to taste them.

Heat spread through her entire body and Emma shoved those thoughts away, focusing on the work in front of her. There was no time to contemplate how she had almost jeopardised her place at this hospital by kissing her boss. Her *married* boss.

'Then page another general surgeon. She's being prepped as we speak,' the nurse behind her said to the person on the other end of the phone.

The nurses wheeled the patient in and Emma began her preparations, getting the age and the weight of her to get the anaesthetic right. A lump appeared in her throat when she inspected the young woman lying on the table. As the nurses around her set up the surgical field, she spotted her belly, protruding in a gentle slope.

'Is she pregnant?' Emma asked no one in particular, even as she opened the patient's file on her tablet.

The ER team had sent her bloodwork to the lab, but the results hadn't come through yet. There were no notes about any examination or ultrasound of her abdomen. Her medication would be different if she were pregnant.

The door swung open and the surgeon walked in, receiving his gloves and gown from the nurse who had been on the phone a few minutes ago. Only when Emma looked up to ask the nurse a question did she notice that they'd paged Mark to perform the surgery.

The scene in the on-call room came back to her mind, and she pushed it away.

'Can I get the ultrasound machine set up?' Emma asked.

The nurse hesitated, looking at Mark. 'What do you need an ultrasound for?'

Emma lifted her tablet, showing the patient's chart. 'The blood panel hasn't come back from the lab yet and I think she might be pregnant. I need to know so I can give her the right type of anaesthesia. We'll also need to set up a foetal monitor to check on the baby during surgery.'

She feared she would have to explain herself further, wasting precious time they didn't have. But to her relief Mark nodded and indicated that the nurse should set it up for her.

'All right, Dr Santos says she needs an ultrasound, so let's turn it around. Time's wasting.'

As the nurses brought in the ultrasound machine, Mark worked on exposing the lower half of her body. The nurse handed her the transducer and Emma took a deep breath as she squeezed some gel onto the patient's abdomen and placed the transducer on it.

The last time she'd performed an ultrasound

on her own had been many years ago, and though she remembered each step, and the principle of it, she suddenly doubted her skill. What if she did it wrong? This wasn't her speciality.

If she had worked at a hospital for her residency, working with pregnant patients would have been a more frequent occurrence. Not for the first time since starting her temporary placement at Attano Memorial, Emma cursed herself for compromising her medical training for the empty promises of Rob. Thanks to her own naivety, she was now riddled with insecurities about something as simple as an ultrasound.

'Maybe we should page OBGYN,' Emma said, and was about to put the transducer down when Mark stepped forward, looking at her with a reassuring spark in his eyes.

'You can do this, Emma. Take a deep breath,' he said, in a voice intended for her ears only. 'Place the transducer beneath her navel and locate the uterus. What do you see?'

Emma swallowed her insecurity and followed the steps. She remembered them from her internship years. Her eyes focused on the screen display of the ultrasound, looking for a foetus. The operating room fell silent around her as she moved the transducer over the patient's abdomen. After a few seconds of intense focus,

Emma pressed the button to freeze the picture and pointed at it.

'There it is.' She put down the handle and wiped the excess gel off the young woman's belly.

Mark nodded, the corners of his eyes crinkling in a half-obscured smile that made her knees weak.

The nurse wheeled the ultrasound machine to the edge of the operating room, and Emma resumed her position at the head of the patient. She prepared the anaesthetic drug and everyone around her kicked into action.

'All right, everyone. There are two lives we're saving today,' Mark said, just as Emma completed the last steps of putting the patient under anaesthetic. She looked over at the monitor showing the patient's vitals, and then she nodded at Mark to begin the surgery.

They worked in unison, with Mark repairing the damage left by the accident while Emma monitored both the mother and child, ensuring they remained low on stress as Mark worked through everything that came up.

The hours passed them by, and only as Mark placed the last stitch did she notice how many had passed. Her tongue clung to the roof of her mouth. She was yearning for a sip of water but she had denied herself, too lost in the procedure. She sighed, the tiredness of the long surgery washing over her.

'Nice work, everybody. Beth, please page OBGYN to make sure they check on the baby,' Mark said beside her. He laid a hand on her shoulder as the people around them shuffled things around. 'That was an excellent call. You saved both their lives today. I know how hectic it can get in the emergency room. It's more efficient to wait for a blood test rather than to do an ultrasound on every single woman who comes through the doors. It's up to us to pay attention.'

Emma smiled as she grabbed her tablet and watched Mark discard his gown and gloves in the bin next to the exit. She pushed the door open with her elbow, and they stepped outside together.

The moment they came out of the OR, Emma felt tension return to her insides as she remembered their encounter in the on-call room. She dared to glance at Mark, wanting to gauge his reaction. Was he flustered, like her? But his face showed nothing of their almost-kiss, and his calm stance as he walked beside her in silence did not betray a single thought.

This was not just her imagination, was it? They had almost kissed. And, more than that, didn't he have a wife? Her eyes darted to his hand, but she didn't spot a ring. Most surgeons decided not to wear jewellery, as they always had to remove it to perform surgery. So his bare finger meant nothing.

Mark didn't look one bit perturbed. Maybe this was him telling her how to deal with the situation. Pretend it had never happened.

'Should I expect to see you join emergency surgeries more often? Not that I'm complaining,' she said, thinking this would be just the thing colleagues would say to each other if they hadn't just almost kissed just a few hours ago.

Mark chuckled. 'I help wherever I can.'

Their eyes locked onto each other's for a second, before his gaze wandered to the wall clock behind her.

'It's longer than I planned on staying, but with one of the general surgeons not being able to come in, I'll probably get paged again.'

They walked into the empty break room and the smell of fresh coffee filled Emma's nose, drawing an awareness of how tired she was.

'Would you rather stay here?' she asked. 'I'll let you have the good bed.'

The memories of their encounter earlier mingled with the snippets of conversation she'd overheard before Georgina's surgery. What was she doing, almost kissing a married man? His proximity had made her forget that important bit of information for a moment. But there was no way of bringing it up. It wasn't any of her business if he had a wife.

Except that he had almost kissed her, too.

'It would shock you to know how often I've chosen to sleep here rather than go home.'

Emma blushed. 'This is my first on-call shift since completing my internship.'

'Your residency must have been mostly nine-to-five, then.' He walked over to the counter and poured himself a coffee, turning around and raising the mug in silent question.

Tempted by the scent, she hesitated a moment before shaking her head. She wouldn't be able to grab any sleep for the rest of her shift. 'Most of the time. Unless a patient needed to be observed overnight—in that case, I would stay. But most of the procedures didn't have long recovery times, and our clients could heal at home.'

Mark plopped down on one of the chairs around the table and she followed suit, sitting down next to him. Her proximity to him made the fine hair along her arms stand on end.

'Clients?' He looked at her with a raised eyebrow, the mug obscuring half of his face.

'Bad habit from working in private practice.'

'Your quick thinking today shows you have lost none of the intuition needed to work at a hospital.'

He lowered the mug, a small smile curling his lips. Emma's stomach lurched under his gaze, and she regretted passing on the coffee. Drinking it would have given her an excuse to break the stare.

'With your talent, I'm curious to know how you ended up at a private practice. Didn't your hospital want you to stay on?'

Emma stared at Mark for a few heartbeats, dreading the turn this conversation had taken. The last thing she wanted to discuss with him was her poor judgement of Rob and her career. Embarrassment flooded every corner of her mind whenever she thought about how ready she had been to give up on her dream for the promise of love. A promise that had crumbled right in front of her when she'd demanded more.

When she had told him that she was going to accept the fellowship offer from Whitebridge, with or without him, he had shown his true colours, trying every tactic to make her feel guilty about choosing her career over him.

But Rob had only ever strung her along, conveniently forgetting about all the times he had put his career first, or the times she had tried to speak to him about their future. And now she was on her own, trying to overcome the insecurities he had foisted on her with his deceit.

'An attending surgeon I'd worked with a lot

asked me to join him at the practice he'd started a couple of weeks before my internship finished. He held all the required licences to teach for the board exam and convinced me to join him.'

She chose her words with care, not wanting anything to show through. Emma would prefer it if Mark thought her choice odd rather than have him knowing the full extent of her naivety.

His hazel eyes darkened as he looked at her, his gaze leaving her face to look at her lips—a small flicker that wasn't lost on her.

Then the low grumble of her stomach cut through the quiet, making her wince. The surgery had gone on for half the night, and the last time she'd had a bite to eat had been before Georgina's surgery. Heat shot into her cheeks, colouring them a soft rouge. That was one of the last sounds she'd wanted Mark to hear.

To add to her embarrassment, his lips parted in a wide grin. 'You're right. It's almost breakfast time.' With one long gulp, he drained the liquid from his mug, putting it back on the table. 'There's a good diner just around the corner. Close enough for us to dash back in case we need to. Let me treat you to some food.'

Breakfast with Mark? Her pulse quickened. She should refuse. Sure, it wasn't unusual for colleagues to have breakfast together, but those colleagues hadn't have an almost-moment in an on-call room a few hours before. Although if what had happened had affected Mark as much as it had her, he wasn't letting on to the fact. Or was this his way of gauging her interest? No, that couldn't be it. He was married, and a man of integrity. He would never betray his spouse like that.

Her attraction to him was one-sided, and it would be better for her if she kept her distance. She should definitely say no. It was the sensible thing to do.

'Yes, I'd like that.'

CHAPTER FIVE

THE ONLY PEOPLE visiting the diner at this hour were people after a night out, looking for a quick breakfast before finding their way home, or people working the night shift at Attano Memorial like themselves.

Mark walked through the door and straight to his regular booth, waving at the waitress as he sat down. He smiled when Emma plopped down opposite him, looking around in curiosity. Despite them having just spent half the night saving a young woman's life, she still looked fresh-faced, her sharp eyes darting around and scrutinising the people in scrubs she saw in the seats.

Even in an unusual setting like that, her eagerness to learn had been the predominant characteristic he'd noticed in her. A trait that the pressure of working with terminally ill patients every day had taken from a lot of his colleagues.

A rueful smile curled his lips when he thought of Emma losing that spark.

With a shake of his head, Mark tried to wave the thoughts intruding upon him away. This time was meant to be about getting to understand his colleague better. His drop-dead gorgeous and intelligent colleague, who was chewing at her lower lip as she studied the menu the waitress had just handed her.

Already familiar with Mark, she didn't bother to hand him one. Instead she just looked at him with her usual sunny demeanour. 'Late-night pancakes?'

'You know me well, Pam,' he said with a chuckle, and looked at Emma as she lifted her eyes from the laminated paper.

'Oh, pancakes! I think I'll go with the same.'

She paused for a moment and then handed the menu back to Pam, who took it from her and vanished through some doors to the kitchen, to get their order sorted out.

'You weren't kidding when you said you spend more time at the hospital than at home. They know what you like to eat here.'

'It gets better.' He chuckled when she raised her eyebrows at him. 'They also know what I like to eat at what specific time. Between midnight and dawn, it's always pancakes.'

Emma laughed at that, as he'd hoped she

would, her green eyes full of sparkling amusement. His eyes trailed down from her face for a moment. He dared to appreciate the view, despite knowing that this was as far as anything would ever go between them. The scrubs made all the staff appear rather uniform, yet somehow she made herself look distinguished.

The vision of her standing in Georgina's room, wearing that dress with the dipping neckline, came back into his mind, tightening his chest and along with it some other parts of his body he hadn't felt in ages.

'Tell me more about your private practice experience,' he said, in a voice he hoped she would think sounded tired rather than thick with the misplaced desire his own thoughts had evoked within him.

When he'd asked her about why she'd done her residency in a private practice rather than in a hospital, Mark had sensed her selecting her words with care about how she might sound. There was something about her experience at her last job that pained her. He could see it written on her face.

'It was a lot different from what my peers experienced in their hospital rotation. I didn't get exposed to a lot of different cases or departments. The patient profiles were quite similar to each other as they were elective cosmetic procedures.' She looked down for a moment, her long lashes obscuring her eyes from view. 'It made studying for the board exam a lot harder, as the questions are varied.'

'Why did you choose that path, then? Seems you understood you were making things harder for you than they needed to be.'

That question had burned in his mind, and he knew the answer would give him some understanding of the intriguing puzzle that was Emma Santos. A part of him urged him to let matters be. But he ignored the small voice. The fire of his own curiosity was demanding to be sated.

Emma hesitated, her eyes dropping from his face for a moment as she took a deep breath. 'I was in love with the man who convinced me to leave the hospital and join him in private practice. When he promised me that the experience would be superior to working at the hospital, I believed him. But it turns out I was wrong.'

Mark raised his eyebrows at the confession, a twinging pain stabbing into his chest. The sudden intimacy as she'd bared her heart to him had caught him off guard, and his pulse quickened. This wasn't the direction he'd wanted the conversation to go, and yet he didn't mind as much as he should. He wanted to know more.

But the pain darkening her face gave him pause, awakening an almost primal protectiveness.

'You're still sharp. Noticing a pregnancy that early on, that attention to detail, that's something that will get you far in your medical career.'

His words seemed to wipe away her pain, and a faint rose colour on her cheeks replaced it, along with an embarrassed smile that drove a searing urge through his body. After his wife's death he'd withdrawn from any kind of female attention, as even the thought of looking at another woman had brought guilt and betrayal to his chest, thickening the darkness he'd woven around himself.

He didn't know what was different about Emma, but something was. Like a breath of fresh air, she was reminding him of the things he denied himself. She was a reminder of what it was like to be attracted to someone again.

Lust.

Desire stirred in his insides from a deep slumber, exciting him more than it should. Concerning him a lot less than he thought appropriate. What had possessed him to invite her to breakfast in the first place?

Mark knew the answer to that question. It was her aura, the warmth she spread through his body just by being near him. She granted him a brief respite from the fog surrounding him.

'I appreciate the compliment,' she said in a quiet voice after Pam had laid the pancakes out in front of them and whisked away at the call of a different patron. 'At the private practice some people were desperate to get their surgeries, despite having factors that might make the procedures riskier. I had to become exceptional at reading people's non-verbal cues so that if they weren't being upfront I would get a sense about it. It's a useful skill for advocating for patients who are already unconscious.'

She paused, grabbing cutlery, and sliced into the first pancake. Mark, holding a fork himself, paused to watch her reaction as the first bite landed in her mouth. Emma's eyes went wide, as if she was surprised at the taste, before she closed them with an appreciative soft moan that vibrated through Mark, shaking up the already growing sensation within him.

'*Meu Deus*, this is delicious,' she said under her breath as she ate another forkful of the fluffy goodness on her plate.

Amused at the way she'd reverted to Portuguese out of pure pleasure, Mark started digging into his own pancakes. His mind wandered, imagining other ways he could bring her so much pleasure she wouldn't be able to help but fall back to her native language.

The thought manifested itself inside him so casually, so non-intrusively. He stopped with his fork halfway to his mouth, wondering what had come over him. He was lusting over his new subordinate like some love-crazed teenager who'd just discovered the opposite sex.

'Are you okay?' she asked, her soft accent mingling with her words, giving them a melody that sounded smooth and distinct.

'Yes, of course,' he lied, and he shook off his contemplations by clearing his throat, desperate to change the topic to something else.

'I'm just feeling tired. I was about to leave before I got paged to the OR,' he said, to bring the topic back to something they could both talk about. Medicine.

'I have to admit I'm excited about my week of on-call shifts at the hospital. I know I can learn a lot,' she said, stopping his thoughts straying from their designated safe space again.

It only took seconds of being within her range for his thoughts to wander, his senses to be filled with awareness for the Brazilian doctor across him.

'That's a helpful attitude to have—especially in a teaching hospital like Attano Memorial.

You're going to have an incredible experience if that's how you think.'

Her smile widened, and his own lips curled upwards in reciprocity. His self-restraint was rendered meaningless when faced with that kind of magnetism. Emma had sidestepped some of his walls, reaching a place within him that had been locked away until meeting her. Getting lost in the attraction, even for one moment, was alluring—and dangerous. It was the place where the lines got blurry...something Mark never permitted.

Was he really ready to move on? What would that even look like? How could he think of someone else when he hadn't been a good enough partner for his late wife?

Mark tried to remind himself of that, of the reasons he had withdrawn from any sort of female attention. But Emma made recalling all his reasons difficult. All he could think of in her presence was the consistent tug of something within his chest.

Emma's heart thudded against her chest in an erratic dance. After their almost-kiss in the on-call room, she'd promised to distance herself from Mark. Instead of doing that, though, she had just opened up about Rob and how he'd tricked her into following him into his practice. She had ended up oversharing, driving an embarrassed heat to her cheeks that had only intensified when she'd noticed his gaze gliding down her body.

He'd made all the fine hair on her nape stand on end as she noticed him checking her out—a picture of pure masculinity and power. Though instead of stopping at some point, and coming back to her face, his eyes had kept going and eventually come to rest on his own hands, lying on the table. His left hand had contracted into a tight fist for a second, before he'd let go of the tension with a slight shake of his head.

It had been a subtle gesture that had reminded her of the conversation she had overheard in the operating room.

'Did you forget to put your wedding band back on?'

The words flew out of her mouth before she could decide whether asking the personal question was a good idea.

Mark's eyes shot up to hers, the glimpse of vulnerability she'd noticed in them just a moment ago vanishing as thick walls appeared around him. Emma knew she had crossed some invisible boundary she shouldn't have touched.

'What makes you think I'm married?' he asked, with caution lacing his words.

Was this where honesty would be the best

policy? She hesitated for a moment, before deciding that she had nothing to lose. Despite the resistance she sensed within her, warning her not to get attached to anyone here, she wanted to know Mark better. For years she had read his research papers and publications, admiring his work and hoping, in the quiet corners of her mind, that he might be the one to discover a cure for the disease that had taken her mother. That might lie dormant in her, too.

'I overheard the conversation between you and Georgina when she was being prepped for her surgery. You must not have noticed me, but I was already there.' This version was close enough to the truth that she didn't feel as if she was deceiving him.

The lines around Mark's jaw tightened for a moment, and she braced herself for a reprimand. His conversation with Georgina hadn't been meant for her ears. Though instead of telling her off he relaxed against the padded back of the booth's bench he sat on and looked at his left hand again before letting out a tired sigh.

'I was married,' he said after a momentary silence, his voice strained with something that could only be fury at her intrusion. 'I'm widowed now.'

Emma's chest tightened at the profound sadness that wove itself through the edges of his words, exposing his wound for her to see.

Her breath caught at the sudden intimacy they shared.

His initial reaction told her he didn't enjoy sharing this part of himself with people, and she remembered the gentle tone he'd used with their patient when comforting her. And now she had prised it out of him to satisfy her own curiosity and nothing else.

Insecurity and regret wrapped themselves around her, creating a tight ball of chaos that wedged itself into the pit of her stomach. 'I'm sorry for bringing it up. I'm sure you don't need me prodding at your wounds.'

The problem was that she wanted to probe further. She wanted to *know* him, to engulf herself in the tantalising aura that came from him. Every time he looked at her, her core contracted, begging her to do something stupid. To reach out and touch him. To pick things up where they'd left off in the on-call room.

His warm breath grazed her cheeks as his scent filled her nostrils—a smell reminding her of pine and clean laundry. Of pleasures untold.

Emma shook her head and got up, unable to deal with his narrowed brown eyes shooting daggers at her. 'I should get going. There could be a surgical case coming in at any moment,' she said.

She was reaching into her pocket to grab her wallet when his hand wrapped around her wrist and pulled her back down onto her seat. A spark travelled down her arm from the spot where Mark touched her, creating fires across her skin as it bounced around before settling in her core.

'Stay,' he said, his dark eyes veiled in an expression she couldn't read.

Her body was no longer her own to command. She sat back down.

'Mentioning Claire helps me bond with patients, so this is probably not the last time you'll hear me talk about her. It's easy for us doctors to appear larger than life to our patients when we talk to them about treatment plans and their options. They need to think of us as capable. But it's scary to put your life into the hands of someone you feel is so different from you. A surgeon talking about his wife is a much more approachable person. It helps to humanise me.'

He stopped for a moment and took a deep breath.

Emma hadn't expected this explanation from him. In the quiet corners of her mind she had wondered why he'd presented himself as married to Georgina when he was widowed. But she had known that wasn't something she could ask her boss. Along with the hundreds of other questions that burned on her tongue.

'I'm sorry for your loss,' she said, remembering that she hadn't expressed her sympathy earlier.

Mark smiled at her. 'Thank you. It's almost two years since she passed away, but she still helps me look after my patients.'

While his tone was serious, she couldn't detect any kind of pain in his words.

'Please—you don't have to explain yourself to me,' she said, with what she hoped looked like a self-assured smile.

Heat coursed through her cheeks. She couldn't believe she had asked these kinds of personal questions of her superior. Nor that he had shared his experience with her without hesitation. Having lost her mother, Emma knew how much it hurt.

Mark leaned back while still looking at her, crossing his arms behind his head, giving her a view of the sculpture that was his upper body. Emma was thankful that she was sitting down, feeling her core ignite as she looked at the man in front of her. Her boss, she reminded herself. Someone who was off-limits.

After everything Rob had put her through, the only thing she would entangle herself in was a no-strings-attached fling before she left this city on her way to a brighter future.

Although she still dreamed of love and romance, of someone to complete her, who wanted to have a family just like her. Despite her chances of bearing her own children being potentially compromised, she hadn't written off building her own family altogether. She knew from the depths of her heart that she and her partner would make it work somehow.

Rob had shown no patience or interest in discussing the topic when she'd approached him about it. Something she now realised was one of the many red flags she had missed, making her wonder what was wrong with her that she hadn't seen the writing on the wall. He couldn't have made it much clearer to her, yet she'd found excuses after excuses for his behaviour. It made her hesitant even to think about her future spouse, or relationships in general. What if she couldn't spot the red flags again?

Maybe a casual encounter would help her with that. Flings were not family material, but neither was her being in Chicago. They were both temporary—a means to an end. She'd come to this place to put her career back on track, as well as to mend her broken heart. Maybe a first step in that was to let go of control. She had never been with anyone outside an actual relationship. This was the first time since med school that she'd been single and not having to work eighty hours a week. Now would be as good a time as any if she wanted to try.

But not with Mark.

He was still her boss, and nothing about him made her think he was a person to indulge in casual affairs. Not when he spoke of his late wife the way he did.

If only he didn't make every inch of her skin tingle with not much more than a fleeting look...

A soft notification tone from her phone interrupted the quiet atmosphere between them, and with an apologetic look she grabbed it from her pocket to look at it. 'One of the interns is asking about local anaesthesia for some stitches in the emergency room.'

Mark raised an eyebrow at that. 'Why are the interns texting you?'

Heat shot up her cheeks under his probing gaze, making her aware of his proximity despite their having an entire table between them. 'I may have given them my number for emergencies.'

Her voice faltered when his eyes scrutinised her with the same precision he used in the operating room. For a moment she was certain

that he could look through her skin and right
into her mind.

'I gave the ER head nurse my number, so she
could contact me in case she needed my help
without making it a 911 page.'

While on call, she knew her primary responsibility was to administer general anaesthetic in
emergency surgeries coming in through the ER,
but Emma wanted to be more useful to her colleagues than that. There weren't usually many
trauma cases throughout the night, and since
she was in the hospital anyway, she wanted to
contribute.

Mark remained quiet for a moment, and then
his lips parted in a smile that turned her insides
into molten lava.

'That is silly of you, because now they won't
stop texting you for every small thing. Admi-
rable, but silly.'

A laugh that sounded a lot more nervous than
she'd wanted it to be escaped her lips as the lava
reached her cheeks. 'At least it will only be for
two months, and then I can ghost them.'

Her comment made him laugh, and he
reached for his wallet, putting a couple of notes
down on the table before standing up. 'Let me
walk you back to the hospital so you can teach
the interns which way to hold the stethoscope.'

Emma's blood hummed with her awareness

of Mark with each step as they strolled back to the hospital, her heart beating against the base of her throat. The man next to her, making butterflies dance up and down her stomach, was award-winning Mark Henderson. A man who regularly graced the covers of different medical journals. Someone who had lost his wife almost two years ago, and who still spoke about her with a gentle fondness in front of their patients.

No matter what kind of pull she felt coming from him, there was no way a man of this calibre would ever be interested in her—casually or otherwise.

'Thanks for the pancakes,' she said when they got to the door of the hospital. 'Now I know where to go when I get hungry.'

They looked at each other for a moment, both of them silent, feeling the pull coming from one another. His eyes narrowed as they wandered down her face, stopping at her mouth. She licked her lips as she noticed their dryness. Her breath caught when Mark leaned in and reached his hand out to her face. A stray strand of hair had fought its way out of the bun, and his fingers brushed over her skin as he pushed it behind her ear.

Her skin was alight with the sparks of his touch. She looked at him. Watched his face come closer to hers again. The moment only lasted a fraction of a heartbeat before he pulled back, his expression shuttered and unreadable...

Mark's chest tightened as he took a step back from Emma, giving himself some room to breathe. That was the second time he had come close to doing something he could never take back. His barriers were up. Yet whenever he got too close to her the resolve within him melted, giving way to the urgent, blazing hot need that he'd denied himself ever since Claire had passed away.

Was that the reason he reacted to her with such strength?

No, something about Emma was different. Unique.

Maybe it was because she would only ever be a temporary addition to his team and his life. Less than two months from now he would have his old anaesthetist back, and whatever traces Emma had left here would soon leave with her. At least that was something he could appreciate.

Was that the reason he'd found himself willing to share so much of his past with her? Mark had not planned on sharing even those few details that had slipped out. His memories of Claire had dropped from his lips before he'd been able to stop them. Something about Emma had been so disarming that his usual defences had failed to kick in.

Mark knew he needed to watch himself as he felt something grow within his chest. It would be best to distance himself. He had shared too much already. There was only one thing he needed to do before he could establish some space between them.

'Since you're working the on-call shift this week, you must be off for a couple of days next week?' he asked, remembering that he'd approved the shift rotation for the oncology department.

Emma nodded after a slight hesitation. 'Yes, that's right.'

'Then let me make good on my promise to show you around Chicago. You shouldn't leave the city before you've had the authentic experience only a Chicagoan can give you.' He smirked. 'And after what you said about deep-dish pizza, I know you need my help.'

He had extended the invitation many hours earlier, but now he was determined to make good on it. Mark was a man of his word.

'I don't want to impose on you,' she said, bringing his thoughts back to reality. 'I appreciate you caring so much.'

'It's no imposition at all.' He paused for a moment, a smile curling his lips. 'I'd ask you to show me around Rochester, should I ever come to visit, but I'm sort of familiar with the place—as you may know.'

She laughed, as he'd hoped she would. A small part of him wanted her to refuse, so he could bow out with no promises broken. But an even larger part wanted to remain close to her, to enjoy the sparks her proximity created within his chest.

It wouldn't lead to anything. Not physical, and definitely not emotional. But it had been a long time since that kind of heat had coursed through his veins, and for a moment he just wanted to enjoy it.

'I guess it would be a shame to leave the city without a proper tour,' she said with a smile, her gaze shifting down his face and stopping at his lips for a moment before coming back up.

A soft scarlet coated her cheeks, and imagining where her thoughts had strayed sent hot blood coursing through his body.

'Great—give me your phone. I'll type in my number so you can text me where to pick you up.'

Emma handed him her phone and he typed in his number before returning it to her. His chest tightened once more when his fingers grazed over her soft skin as he handed the device back to her.

He waved at her as she turned and walked through the door, smiling when she looked back as if to have just one more look at him before she vanished around the corner.

With his heart beating against his chest at an unsteady pace Mark walked to his car, his mind reeling from the last couple of hours. Something had shifted inside him. He knew the wise thing would be to turn away. He would never be available on an emotional level, and she didn't strike him as someone who liked things casual.

With a drawn-out sigh, he closed the car door and started driving. He would show her around Chicago, and they would have a decent time talking about the city and the work they had in common. He'd said he would show Emma around, and that was what he was going to do. After that, he would distance himself.

Desire made his pulse quicken, but he couldn't go there with anyone—even if he kept emotion out of it. But at the very least he'd learned that this part of him was not lost completely.

CHAPTER SIX

EXHAUSTION CREPT INTO every corner of her body when Emma came out of her last on-call shift, and only with a supreme effort did she get to her flat before passing out on her bed, too tired to shower or have a bit of food.

Despite being there only for emergency surgeries, she'd found herself busier than she'd thought, assisting the more inexperienced doctors with general tasks. As wiped out as this left her, the sleep that enveloped her was an excellent one, her feelings of accomplishment letting her drift off into a relaxed slumber.

Until a certain Dr Handsome sneaked his way into the adventures she was dreaming of.

Emma woke up several hours later with her sense of accomplishment gone, replaced by a more heated, pinching feeling in her core as the visions of her dreams faded away. With an annoyed grunt, Emma threw her covers off and opened the curtains to look outside for a moment.

The sun was shining high in the sky without a single cloud in sight. Of course it would be the nicest day Chicago has seen in ages, when she wanted it to rain and thunder. A storm would be a more appropriate representation of what was going on within herself when she thought about who she was going to spend the afternoon with.

Dr Mark Henderson—famous surgeon, and the reason she'd come to Chicago—had asked her out on a date. No, Emma reminded herself as her stomach lurched. There had been no mention that this was a date of any sort. This was nothing more than a professional courtesy extended from the department head to his newest employee. Anything else would be inappropriate.

Although it was the 'anything else' part that made Emma's pulse quicken. Could there be more behind his invitation, or was she constructing something in her mind that didn't exist? There had been that moment in the diner last week, when an unexpected closeness had enveloped them as they'd shared things with each other they both didn't talk about under normal circumstances.

Her heart squeezed tight within her chest when she remembered the hurt in his eyes as he'd revealed his wife's death to her. It had only been visible for a second before he'd regained control of his expression, his eyes shuttering right in front of her before she could reach out.

I'm leaving soon. Should be at your place in thirty minutes.

Emma stared at his text, her stomach turning itself into a knot as she read the words, hearing them in his voice. Her fingers hovered above her phone, and she contemplated whether she should cancel. She couldn't deny how drawn to Mark she was, on more than just a professional level, and it was that magnetism that gave her pause. Along with the way he had looked at her when they'd almost kissed, turning her insides to liquid fire.

After their conversation in the diner Emma had called her cousin Livia to talk through some of her thoughts, careful not to reveal too much or the entire family would be on her case about it. It was Livia who kept encouraging her to 'let loose'. She had also been the one to help her through her break-up with Rob.

What Emma hadn't mentioned was that the man who'd caught her attention was her superior. She knew she should know better than to get involved with her boss.

See you soon.

He isn't married.

Emma's heart skipped a beat when that intrusive voice echoed through her mind. Why should she care? His not being married didn't make him less off-limits. In fact, his having lost his wife made him even more off-limits. He hadn't specified how she'd died, and Emma hadn't wanted to ask after he had just shared so much with her. But she had her own shadows of mortality chasing her. She could be sick herself, and live not much longer than her mother had.

The hurt written on Mark's face had been the same hurt she had seen so many times in her father's face. She refused to put anyone through that. Emma would get the genetic test before she started to date again. And, since she had convinced herself to get the test after her fellowship was over, she had a timeline to work with. Nothing serious until her time in Rochester was up.

She looked at the time on her phone screen and jumped, cursing at how much time she had just wasted daydreaming when she needed to get ready.

Most of her belongings were still in the boxes she had used to bring them from San Francisco. With her locum tenens gig only lasting two months, she hadn't bothered to unpack anything or to get too comfortable in the apartment. She would be out of here before she knew it, and would rather spend the energy of home decoration on her flat in Rochester.

The sole exception was the two large potted plants standing on a windowsill. They were exotic plants, native to her home in Brazil. Caring for them helped with the occasional pang of homesickness Emma experienced whenever too much time passed without seeing her family.

She dug through a box with clothes in it, finding a knee-length summer dress with a high neck and a blue floral print. Nice and appropriate. She threw it on, slipped into her heels, and by the time she'd tamed her curls the doorbell rang, making her jump.

Her heart beat against the base of her throat with such erratic ferocity that she was certain that if Mark looked at her collarbone, he would see her pulse. Why was she reacting to him with such yearning when she knew that there wasn't anything between them? Was she that starved for attention? There were more than enough reasons for her to be cautious rather than excited.

Shutting those thoughts away, Emma took a deep breath and opened the door. Her breath caught in her throat when she saw Mark leaning against her doorframe with a small smile on his soft-looking lips.

'Olá,' he said, oblivious to the flames licking across her skin.

'Você fala português?' Upon hearing the familiar greeting, she reverted to her native language, raising her eyebrows in surprise.

Mark chuckled and raised his hands with a shake of his head. 'I assume you asked if I speak Portuguese, and I regret to say no. But I used to work closely with a Brazilian physician a few years back, and picked up a few bits and pieces along the way.'

'Oh, so I'm not your first Brazilian doctor?' she said, unsure what had driven her to verbalise that thought.

An amused spark entered Mark's eyes as he looked at her. 'Would you believe me if I told you she meant nothing to me?'

Emma looked at him in surprise, feeling the blood rush to her cheeks at his tone. Of all the things he could have said, she hadn't expected him to be flirtatious.

'Oh, so I'm just one in a series of many?' She tried her best to sound outraged, but couldn't keep the playful edge out of her voice.

Mark clasped his hands over his chest, as if struck by her words. 'She was part of the team looking after Claire when she got sick.'

Her illness had required an entire team to look after her? Emma made a note of that as she tried to uncover more about his past without the risk of things getting too personal. For a moment she wondered if it had been cancer. It would make sense, given his obvious dedication to the oncology department at Attano Memorial.

He hesitated a moment, and Emma could see him considering his next words.

'You look lovely,' he said eventually, and those three words created a cascade of fireworks across her entire body, exploding everywhere and leaving a pulsating warmth behind.

'Thank you,' she said, cringing as her voice faltered for a moment. 'I've never seen you in street clothes before. I was half expecting you to wear dark green scrubs.'

He laughed at her quip and led her down the stairs, opening the car door for her as they reached the vehicle, leaving her to glance around for only a second before he took the driver's seat.

'So where are we headed?' she asked, desperate for him to drive so he would take his eyes off her. His glances, along with his scent, were filling her head with pictures of her steamy dream, and fire was engulfing her core.

'There are some food stalls along the waterfront at Millennium Park. It's quite a popular place for both locals and tourists, with a magnificent view of the harbour and a curious structure people like to call The Bean.'

Fifteen minutes later, Emma understood what he meant. Rising tall in front of her was a sculpture in the shape of a bean, its two ends standing on the floor, forming a gate large enough that people could walk underneath it. The Cloud Gate—which was the actual name of the sculpture—was made of a mirror-like material, reflecting everything around it.

Emma circled it with wide eyes, watching as the reflection of the surrounding city changed as she walked farther. Mark stepped up to her, pointing her towards the harbour, where she could already spot a few food stalls and a large group of tables and benches where people were enjoying their meals.

To her relief—and it *was* relief, not regret, Emma told herself—Mark kept a respectful distance between them. Although despite the several feet separating them, she could still feel the electric current of their tension skipping between their bodies as they walked together. Mark's entire demeanour was calm and unyielding…only the spark in his eyes betraying his thoughts.

'Is it time for some rib tips?' she asked as they walked close to one stall.

The veiled expression on his face made a

shiver crawl down her spine and heat reach for her cheeks.

'I would recommend that—and I would hope you'd trust me over some strangers on the internet,' he said, with a chuckle following his words that made her shake at her centre.

After the intense moment they'd shared in the on-call room, a little more than a week ago, Emma had thought she'd made it clear to herself that this attraction she was giving in to was unacceptable and downright irresponsible. He was her boss. She couldn't let her primal needs override what was the career opportunity of a lifetime.

'You were right about the pancakes, so I trust your recommendations.'

She pushed the intrusive thoughts away and focused on what was important—making a lasting impression on Mark that was based on her competencies as a doctor and not the fluttering of desire within her centre. Her attraction to him would only make things more complicated, and difficult things were at the bottom of the list of things Emma wanted.

Now that she knew about his late wife, keeping distant had become even more important. She brought her own baggage in a potential cancer diagnosis. Something that she couldn't put on anyone—especially not someone like Mark, who had already seen enough suffering to last him a lifetime.

After ordering their food, Mark led her away from the stalls and tables surrounding them, settling down on a bench overlooking the harbour. Lake Michigan sparkled in the afternoon sun as if covered with a million tiny diamonds.

'I didn't think a place here could remind me so much of Rio de Janeiro,' she said as she looked out on the water, remembering the white beaches and the glistening waters of her home.

Mark looked at her with a smile. 'Do you miss home?'

Emma poked around in her food as she considered his question. It was more personal than she wanted it to be. After sharing so much of her pain around Rob with him last week, she wanted to be careful not to breach their professional boundaries again. If only he didn't make it so easy to open up.

'Home is such an abstract concept,' she said after a few moments of silence. 'I've always considered home to be wherever I am. But I miss Brazil sometimes. When I was growing up, it seemed almost impossible to leave. And I'm used to having my family surround me. Going from that to being all by myself is still strange sometimes.'

'I wonder what that must be like.'

Emma looked up from her food, quickly enough to catch a glimmer of longing in his eyes before it faded. 'Do you not have a family here?' she asked.

He shook his head. 'My parents are making their best out of their retirement years. Every couple of months they're in a different country, so we don't see each other much. Claire's sisters used to visit her a lot at our place in Rochester...' He paused for a moment, as if thinking about his next words. 'It was nice to have them around. I guess I understand what you mean.'

They looked at each other, and the fine hair on her arms stood on end as she recognised the glimmer of unexpected closeness in his eyes. She got the sense that he wasn't used to sharing these kinds of thoughts with the people around him. That he had shared some of his memories surrounding Claire with her sent a warmth cascading through her.

'But you grew up here in Chicago?' She wasn't sure, but the way he spoke about the city made it sound as if he'd spent a lot of time here.

He nodded, his eyes drifting back to the lake with a fond smile. 'My parents had a family practice in one of the suburbs. They were thrilled when I started med school. Less so when they realised I wasn't going to take over the practice.'

Eyes wide in surprise, Emma tilted her head. 'You don't have any siblings to share the spotlight?'

Mark shook his head. 'I had an older brother, but I never met him. He died only a few weeks after he was born. I was a bit of a surprise baby to my parents when they had given up.'

'Oh, no, I'm so sorry.' Emma's thoughts went to her cousins, and how each one of them played an important part in her life. She couldn't imagine losing any of them.

'Don't be. I was born many years later, with extra-large shoulders to carry the expectations my parents had for me. Maybe that's something I learned to appreciate with Claire and all her sisters. They had each other to lean on when they were growing up.' He paused, a wistful smile on his lips. 'That closeness didn't stop as they grew older, and they were there to support us when she got sick.' Stillness settled between them as his voice trailed off, and eventually he cleared his throat. 'What about you?'

Emma was also an only child, though she wasn't sure if it was by choice or not. She knew there had been complications during her birth, but she'd never asked for more details. By the time she'd been old enough to care, her mother had been diagnosed with Gardner Syndrome and it hadn't seemed to matter any more.

'No siblings either—though my cousins filled that gap for me. We all lived on the same street and we could walk into each other's houses whenever we wanted. It's something I'd like my own kids to have as well.'

'You want your children to grow up in Brazil?'

Mark raised an eyebrow at her, with a curious spark in his eyes that caused a flutter in her chest. How had they got onto such a personal topic? This was the exact opposite of the detached conversation she'd wanted to have.

'I guess I do... I haven't thought much about it. Children are very much only a concept at the moment.' She paused, heat climbing up to her face. 'What about you? Would you be happy to have a family here in Chicago?'

The question left her lips before she could think about what she was saying, her curiosity getting the better of her. What a stupid thing to ask a widower—as if he hadn't had plans and watched them all fall apart when his wife died.

Mark remained quiet for a moment, his hand going up to his face to tap against his chin. 'Not something I've thought about since Claire died. When she fell ill, we had to have a serious discussion about it...with the chemotherapy and all.'

'Oh, she had cancer?' The confirmation of

her suspicion didn't make the information any easier to swallow. Although it explained a lot about his work ethic, and how much he cared for each patient. 'It mustn't be easy to watch your patients struggle through the same steps.'

Mark sighed, shook his head, and let his eyes drift back to her. 'It rarely is, but it comes with the job.'

His gaze still lingered on her, and awareness of his proximity flooded her senses as she tilted her head to look back out on the water.

'If you're close to your family, why did you come to the States?' he asked.

'I always wanted to be a doctor. My family had little means, so I needed to have the grades and some kind of scholarship to get me to my goal. I threw everything I had at it, and landed myself a place at med school in San Francisco.' She paused for a moment and laughed. 'When my mother passed away I was almost ready to quit and stay in Brazil. But my father wouldn't let me. He said he wouldn't let me make decisions I would later regret because of the grief we were going through together.'

A flutter of an expression moved over Mark's face, the moment too short for her to recognise it. 'You remain close with your father?' he asked.

Emma nodded with a big smile. 'Very much. I

had just turned twenty when my mother passed away, but even before that my dad and I were supporting each other through the procedures and the hospital visits. You've seen it yourself how people band together in crisis. Even though he had lost his wife, he made sure that I came through the other side.'

'I'm glad he did,' Mark said after a pause, in a low voice that made her insides hum with awareness of him.

The gentleness of his tone took her by surprise. He was genuine, clearly meaning what he said. But what did that mean?

She looked at him for a moment, her eyes wide, before dropping her gaze to her hands, the tension it created too intense. She was afraid she was reading too much into his intentions. He was a talented surgeon who liked to surround himself with passionate people. There was no reason for her to believe his interest in her went beyond any professional boundaries.

Before Emma could contemplate his words any further, he stood up and extended his hand towards her. 'Care for some more walking? I'd like to show you the flower gardens surrounding the fountain at the centre of the park.'

She took his hand and got up from the bench, her skin tingling where they touched. Their gazes meshed for a moment. Her body reacted to his proximity, her senses humming with an awareness of how close they were. His expression softened, his thumb brushing over her fingers as she stepped closer to him.

Emma lifted her chin as he stood firm in place, a curious spark lighting up his dark brown eyes. Her breath caught in her throat when he leaned in. Was he going to kiss her?

'I like…flowers.'

Those were the only words manifesting in her mind that were okay to say in such proximity to her boss. A myriad of other things rolled around in her head, but none of them were professional or even appropriate.

Her words seemed to snap Mark out of his strange trance. He blinked, and the next moment the strange curiosity in his gaze faded, replaced by the impenetrable barriers she was used to seeing.

He stepped away from her and they started walking down the sunny paths of the park. Heat was blooming inside her chest, despite her mind telling her that this had already gone too far.

When they entered the gardens she almost immediately forgot all her reservations as she marvelled at the beautiful flowerbeds that were laid out around an impressive rococo fountain. Lush green rose bushes lined the twisted pathways, weaving themselves through the pristine grass. Every single leaf looked as if it had received special attention from the gardener, carefully manicured so the flowers could present their best side to the visitors admiring them.

Emma had grown up in Rio de Janeiro, far away from the rainforest, but it had always held a special place in her heart. When she was younger, she had convinced her parents to take a trip to Manaus, so she could see the Amazonian forest with her own eyes. That trip had sparked an appreciation for plants. While she wasn't a talented gardener herself, she still kept plants around her that reminded her of the tropical forest of her home country.

'Que lindo!' she said under her breath as they kept on walking, occasionally stopping for her to take some pictures. 'My cousins are going to love these.'

Mark smiled at that. 'I noticed your apartment was mostly plants and boxes. Do you already have a place to stay in Rochester?'

Emma blushed at the thought that he'd seen her dishevelled flat. 'No, I haven't—though it would be a good idea to start looking soon. Any recommendations?'

Mark watched Emma's expression as they strolled through the park, an intense feeling of longing growing within his chest as a faint rosepink coloured her dark honey-toned cheeks. His hands twitched, wanting to reach out and feel the warmth that her flesh promised. But he knew he couldn't go there.

Her family dynamic sounded unfamiliar and intriguing to him. Unlike her, he'd grown up by himself. Although through Claire and her sisters he had witnessed a similar dynamic to the one Emma had described. Her family had never been far away when they'd needed them.

Growing up had been very different for him. His parents were doctors, too, and had prioritised their careers over a big family. Not that he hadn't been loved or cared for. They had been amazing and inspiring parents to him. But the closest Mark had ever got to having an extended family was the staff at his parents' clinic. His parents had always encouraged him, but would they have pushed him out of the darkness the way Emma's father had done for her?

Her father's words had reached him in a strange way he couldn't quite explain. After her mother's death, he hadn't let Emma follow a destructive path out of sheer grief. Was that what Mark had done? He had moved on, forgotten about the life he and Claire had planned before she fell ill. But fragments of the past followed him around, always reminding him of his failure. As a doctor he hadn't been able to find the path towards a cure, and as a husband he hadn't been present enough to be there when she'd needed him in her last moments.

Those shadows still chased him, though he had noticed their relentless pursuit fading, giving way to other things. Such as the desire and attraction that had set his blood ablaze the moment Emma had opened the door to her apartment.

Mark had readied himself that morning with cool detachment, not wanting to let Emma glimpse any more of his past than she already had. But right now his body and mind were in a constant battle for dominance. And the warmth from her touch when she'd grasped his hand, held out to help her off the bench, had trickled into his arm, disturbing his already uneven balance with a rush of desire.

He'd been close to crossing his self-imposed line at that moment, and as he watched her marvel at the fountain he was edging towards it again. The soft curve of her lips filled him with desire, and all he could think of was to steal a taste of them.

Mark forced himself to look away. His thoughts turned to her question, and then memories of his time in Rochester surfaced in his mind. Memories he guarded close.

He and Claire had lived near the Whitebridge

Institute as they'd been working there before Claire had got her life-altering diagnosis. Back then, he'd still believed they were going to survive the disease, putting all his effort into the research that would save her and millions of other people's lives. Something that remained his mission to this day.

'We stayed close to the clinic. Claire wanted to live in a house with a garden, so she could grow vegetables. I don't know where she found the time with the schedule we were keeping,' he said, remembering the many jars of pickled vegetables filling their cupboards. 'Our proximity to the hospital allowed her to escape her room more often than other patients.'

Emma stared out onto the water of the fountain before looking back at him with a small smile. 'Do you miss the research opportunities at Whitebridge? I notice your name hasn't appeared as much as it used to in the journals I read.'

'I'm proud of what I've built here in Chicago,' he said. And then he contemplated his answer. 'After everything that happened I couldn't stick around. I miss the research, and the people I worked with, but I didn't have the heart to stay.'

With her question, she had found a weak spot without even trying. Not being able to do as much research as he'd used to was the price he'd paid when he left Rochester. It hurt to admit it, but he hadn't been strong enough to stay there. Wherever he went, his surroundings had reminded him of his broken promise and his crushed heart.

What caught Mark by surprise was how easy it was for him to admit all this now. Not only that, but it was also freeing to unburden himself in front of someone who understood where he came from. While he had worked with his staff at Attano Memorial for the better part of two years now, he had never found himself in a situation where he could speak about Claire in such detail.

They moved away from the fountain, their feet choosing their own path as they focused on their conversation. Eventually, they stood near the waterfront again.

'Which research papers have you read?' he asked.

Emma chuckled. 'All of them. When my mother was diagnosed, her oncologist recommended I read up on your work when she realised I was attending med school.' She blushed as she looked away. 'Your papers on pain management in cancer patients were inspiring.'

'You found the papers inspiring?'

Mark knew his words were bordering on teasing, but he couldn't help himself. Despite being content with his move, he enjoyed hearing that his research still held relevance for people. Or was it the fact that it was Emma who'd enjoyed his work that sparked the warm feeling in his chest?

The blush blooming on her cheek was exquisite, and Mark fought the urge to reach out to her. He already knew how soft her skin was to his touch, and he craved more. Much more.

'And now that I know why you worked so hard on your research I'm even more impressed. You wanted to save your wife.'

A noble but misguided notion. He'd wanted to save Claire and their future together. But when he'd realised he couldn't, he'd wanted to spare himself the pain of her death. Though he couldn't bring himself to admit that in front of Emma. He had already shared so much of his past with her. The details had escaped his lips before he'd been able to think of a reason not to share them. Most concerning of all was how much lighter he'd felt after it. Almost free to appreciate the yearning feelings developing in his chest.

What was it about Emma that made him unable to keep things professional? Her admiration flattered him, but other women had approached him with similar words and hadn't caught his interest. It couldn't just be the fact that she would leave soon. Or was it the only way he dared to feel like a red-blooded man again? Because he knew it would lead nowhere?

He stared out at the water of the lake again and sensed her eyes drifting away, joining his in looking straight ahead.

'It's a lot warmer than I expected it to be so close to the border,' she said, and he could almost hear the smile accompanying her words before tilting his head to see it. The melody of her accent was tinting her every word.

'Is this the first time living this far north for you?' he asked.

She nodded. 'I'm glad I made it up here in summer, though. I wonder what it would have been like later in the year.' Emma paused for a moment, hesitating before speaking her next words. 'I've never had a cold winter.'

Mark smiled at the confession and tried to recall the winters he had spent studying in Minnesota. 'You'll be in for a surprise. Just make sure you get some UV lights to combat seasonal affective disorder. I would also recommend chocolate, but for overall nutrition, light would be better.'

Emma laughed at that, her lips parting in a sensual smile that drove all his blood to the lower half of his body. How had they turned a discussion about the weather into sexy banter?

'If you write me a prescription for chocolate, do you think my health insurance will cover my grocery bill?'

Mark shrugged, desire coiling itself around his chest in a tight knot that took his breath away. If the weather wasn't a safe topic, he needed to talk about something else.

'What made you choose anaesthetics as a speciality?' They had spoken about her career before, but he'd never asked her why she had chosen that path. Or why she wanted to deviate from it now.

Emma swallowed, her lashes fluttering as she cast her eyes down for a moment before she looked at him again. 'When I started med school I thought I was going into surgery the second I could get my hands on a surgical internship. But then, halfway through, my mother's condition got a lot worse.'

In an instinct to comfort her, he reached out, grabbing her hand and squeezing it for support as her voice trembled at the memory. She smiled, but the pain was still visible in her deep green eyes.

'The team that took care of my mother was so dedicated to her care, and to making sure her last moments were as peaceful as they could be. That's when I decided I wanted to work around pain management, so when anaesthetics came up in our studies, it seemed like the perfect fit.'

Emma paused for a moment as if to compose herself—or maybe to relive the moment in her memories. Mark couldn't tell, nor could he explain the ache blossoming in his chest, but the display of such delicate vulnerability gave way to something inside him. His mouth went dry at the familiarity of the pain she was so openly showing him, and his heart stuttered in his chest.

'So why move into emergency medicine now?'

'I wasted my time on someone who wasn't serious about me, who compromised my career.' She paused for a moment to shake her head in disbelief. 'Instead of learning from the surgeons at a hospital, I got stuck witnessing the same procedures over and over again, with nothing to challenge my mind. I needed a change, and now I find myself in a situation where I have no more time to waste. I'm not getting back the time that I lost, but at least now I can focus on doing what I want…'

Her voice trailed off and Mark looked at her. She had opened up about the man she'd been in a relationship with before coming to Chicago before. A fact that gave rise to different emotions inside his chest—none of which were appropriate for him to indulge.

Mark was furious at the mistreatment Emma had suffered at his hands. The hurt shone through her voice each time she mentioned him. That she'd had her trust abused like that speared white-hot anger coupled with an irrational protectiveness into his body. But what affected him even more was the vulnerability with which she'd laid her heart bare. To him. A virtual stranger. Unlike Mark, she possessed the courage to let him see her hurt, because it was a part of her story.

Something inside him shifted at that thought.

Emma chuckled into the silence. 'I thought I was shooting for the stars when I applied to the programme at the Whitebridge Institute, and it still hasn't sunk in yet.'

'From what I've seen of you so far, I know you'll be an invaluable asset to the programme. Being surrounded by so many passionate medical professionals was the experience of a lifetime for me, and I still lean on the relationships I built there to this day.'

'I want to be part of a bigger thing, and I hope this choice will help me accomplish that.'

Even before Claire's death Mark had declared cancer the enemy of his life, vowing to work hard to find a cure and to help people survive. Emma—just like him—had experienced loss and transformed it into something noble. Into a new purpose to dedicate themselves to. They were cut from the same cloth.

He reached out, unable to stay his hand any longer, brushing his fingers against her cheek, relishing the exquisite feel of silken skin beneath them.

This road would not lead Mark anywhere he should go, but he wanted to go there regardless. Emma reached a place in him that had lain dormant and obscured for the last two years. He wasn't sure what it was, or how she had managed it.

When had he let his guard down long enough for her to slip through?

It didn't matter. His soul felt weightless for the first time, and he wanted to enjoy it for as long as it would last.

He looked at her, at the dark green eyes wide in a puzzled expression, her lips slightly open as if inviting him to follow the thoughts forming in his hungry mind. The voice in his mind cautioning him faded away as he closed the remaining gap between them. His fingers wandered down underneath her chin, angling her face towards his as he captured her mouth with his, enrapturing them both in a kiss.

* * *

Emma watched as Mark came closer, her insides turning into liquid fire as the tension became unbearable. Then their lips touched and fireworks ricocheted across her skin, setting fire to every nerve in her body.

Unable to resist—or to even to recall a reason why she shouldn't surrender to Mark with her entire being—Emma leaned in as her longing for him took over. His mouth brushed against hers with a gentleness that was at odds with the fire roaring within her. Yet the softness of the moment was exactly the way she had imagined it since their almost-kiss in the on-call room. It was a kiss filled with promise and suppressed desire, ready to break through the restraints she had been bound with.

Her hands came to rest on his chest, and she melted against him as he pulled her closer into his embrace. As he deepened their kiss her senses were overloaded, and when his hands wandered down her back the fire across her body roared with an intensity Emma hadn't known she could feel.

Sense tried its best to pierce the thick cloud of need as she gave herself to Mark. He pulled back for a moment, his dark eyes peering into hers. His hand rested on her face, and he stroked her cheek with his thumb before he pulled her into another kiss that left her catching her breath. What was she doing? This wasn't some nameless surgeon to fulfil her need for a fling. No, she was kissing Mark Henderson himself. The man whose research she had spent countless hours reading. Her boss.

Emma didn't know if he could sense her thoughts, or if his own mind had caught up with what they were doing, but Mark broke away from her with a moan that gave her an idea of how hot the desire was running in his veins.

He looked at her for a moment, his expression veiled, not letting her see what was going through his head. His hands let go of her and he stepped away, creating some space between them.

'I'm sorry. I shouldn't have done that,' he said, rubbing the light stubble on his cheek with his hand. His chest was heaving, the connection they had just a couple of seconds ago still visible.

Emma opened her mouth, searching her mind for an appropriate response, but no words manifested themselves. She shouldn't have done it either, for so many reasons that she needed both her hands to count them. Mark was her superior. This was something that could disrupt her job. The career that she had just saved from the ashes of her last relationship. But even more than that were their personal circumstances, which ruled out any kind of emotional attachment.

He had lost his wife to cancer, and now dedicated his life to fighting the disease. It was a fight she wanted to join him in, with her own looming condition a constant shadow at the back of her mind. For that reason alone she could not let herself get attached to Mark.

What if she got ill? He wouldn't want to burden himself with another sick person in his life. Something she didn't want either.

This was only ever going to end in a calamitous disaster. Emma knew that. Yet she felt the space Mark had put between them in the pit of her stomach, and her entire body was yearning to get back to the kiss they'd shared. To take it even further. Every nerve in her body sent the same signal, wanting to get lost in the luscious feeling of his body pressed against hers.

'I—' she began, but was interrupted by an urgent beeping coming from Mark's phone.

He pulled it out of his pocket and looked at the screen. A frown appeared on his face. 'I'm being paged for an emergency,' he said with a sigh.

'Go. I can find my way back home,' she said when she saw his hesitant look.

'No, I should take you home first.' Mark's

eyes wandered to the message on his phone again, his fingers hovering over the screen to send a reply.

'You'll lose too much time.'

Mark looked at her for a moment, his expression a mixture of longing and regret, but he nodded as he put his phone away. 'You're right. Thank you for understanding.'

Emma shrugged. 'It's a doctor's life—nothing I'm not familiar with.' She tried to lighten the mood, though the smile on her face felt almost frozen in place.

He looked at her for a moment, his hands hovering by his sides, as if he was deciding what to do next. Eventually he gave her a small wave as he left in the direction they had come from only a couple of hours ago.

With an enormous sigh, Emma let herself fall onto a bench nearby, burying her face in her hands. What had just happened? Had she really kissed Mark, the head of the oncology department at the hospital? Of all the things she'd expected to happen on her brief stint in Chicago, this hadn't been one of them. How could she have let her impulses get the better of her?

A casual fling was one thing—but not with this man. The memory of the kiss came back to her...the softness of his touch raising the hair on her arms into tiny goosebumps. Their connection was undeniable, despite her having so many reasons to forget this day had ever happened.

'Why couldn't it have rained today?' she mumbled into her hands, before letting out another sigh.

By the time she looked up the park already seemed a lot darker. She didn't know how much time she had spent lamenting her poor decision-making, but it was time to get home. A warm shower and loads of ice cream would help her make sense of the turmoil brewing within her chest.

CHAPTER SEVEN

MARK'S NIGHTS WERE filled with pictures of Emma. Her soft lips trailing over his collarbone. Her hands exploring every inch of his body. His taut length finding sweet release within her.

He woke up each morning, banishing the thoughts of something that hadn't even happened. Wouldn't happen ever.

Mark could not believe he had let it get as far as it had. Staring at his bedroom ceiling, he waited for the heavy blanket of guilt and obligation to descend on him like it always did. But it never came, leaving him instead with heat spreading from his chest to his groin.

Was this the last step he had been waiting for? All the support groups and the literature around grieving told him that the pain would fade away. That fond memories would replace it instead. His failings as a husband were still present, though.

He and Emma had spent the last two weeks

avoiding each other after what had happened in the park, and while he knew their distance was for the best, he couldn't get her out of his head.

How could that be? The allure coming from Emma was unlike any attraction he had experienced with any woman ever since he'd met his late wife. The intensity of their connection was exhilarating. And deeply concerning. It was as if she saw through the surgeon persona he had constructed and stared right at the man he'd used to be. The man he might even become again one day.

And, as much as the desire wanted to wreak havoc throughout his body, he couldn't give himself permission to give in to anything emotional. The one chance he'd had at a happily-ever-after had died with Claire. But what if this wasn't emotional? What if this was a purely physical attraction between two consenting adults?

The thought kept rolling around in his head without any apparent purpose or destination.

Was that really something he wanted to consider? He'd only ever been with one woman, having met Claire right after high school. Mark wouldn't even know how to start that conversation.

Giving up on falling back to sleep, Mark rolled out of bed and went about his morning routine before getting into the car and driving to the hospital. He had already helped with several emergency surgeries this week, and reached the maximum amount of hours the hospital's policy permitted him to work.

Luckily for him, he had found a loophole in that policy. While he wasn't allowed to work at the hospital, he was permitted to spend time at the free clinic that the Alexander Attano Foundation ran. The clinic was always understaffed, with the hospital often being unable to free up more than one or two physicians to help, so he relished the thought of spending his time in such a meaningful way.

The nurse managing the front desk sighed with relief when he walked in. 'I was praying we would see you today. We only have one other physician here. They said they were going to send someone else in a bit, as one of the surgery boards is light today, but she might need some training—so who knows what kind of intern they're sending us?'

Mark took the tablet she was offering him with a raised eyebrow, looking through the patients who were waiting to be seen. The nurses had already asked their first diagnostic questions, triaging the patients by severity. The first five all needed stitches.

He walked up to the first patient. 'Good morning, Ms Scott. My name is Dr Henderson. The nurses tell me you've come in with a cut on your arm. Would you mind if I had a look?'

The older woman nodded and Mark put on his gloves and lifted her arm so he had a better view of the wound.

'I slipped while trimming my hedges,' the woman explained as he continued his inspection. 'My grandson tells me he'll do it for me when he gets home from school, but I don't want to trouble him.'

Mark looked up, a soft smile curling his lips. 'I think your grandson just worries about you, Ms Scott.'

She shook her head. 'Please, call me Lucy.'

'All right, Lucy. This is superficial, but we'll need to apply some stitches before we bandage you up.' He got up from the stool he'd sat on. 'I'm going to grab the supplies we need and then we'll get started.'

As he walked to the supply cupboard to grab a suture kit, the figure standing at the front desk with the admissions nurse caught his attention. His chest tightened when he recognised Emma—all soft curves and beauty, even in the uniform scrubs she wore—talking to the nurse sitting behind the screen.

The nurse made eye contact with Mark and waved him over. Emma turned to see who she was waving at, and he noticed the slight blush spreading through her cheeks. Memories from that day two weeks ago came rushing back into his conscious mind, the lust she evoked in him clawing at him again the moment their eyes met.

His reaction to her was visceral, eluding any kind of self-control he tried to exert on himself. Two weeks had not been enough to cool anything between them.

'Theresa has sent Dr Santos down here to help. Could you show her around and split up the current patients? Once you get through them, I'll admit more for the day,' she said when Mark stepped closer to the desk.

Steeling himself, he turned to Emma. The last thing he needed was any of the staff to pick up on the tension thrumming between them. He asked her to follow him with a nod, not wanting to say anything until they were out of earshot. He didn't plan on having any kind of confrontation. What had happened the other day had been nothing more than a lapse of judgement as he rediscovered what it was like to be attracted to a woman again.

The silence between them grew, and unspoken words hung between them.

'What's your experience with general medicine?' he asked to break the silence as he walked them to the supply closet. Best not voice what had happened between them, or he might find himself in a similar situation again.

'I did a lot of patient care in my intern years. Less so in residency. I'm confident in my diagnostic skills, though,' she replied.

Mark believed her, but he was hearing a slight edge in her voice. The tension between them picked up the second he was near enough to touch her, as his body remembered what she'd felt like pressed against him. Was she thinking about their kiss as well?

'Most cases here tend to not be too severe, though today we have a couple of wounds that need to be stitched. How comfortable are you with those?'

He grabbed a suture kit and turned around to look at her. Emma bit on her lower lip and looked down, her long lashes obscuring her eyes for a moment. The curve of her mouth drew his gaze, and remembering the softness of them against his own drove the blood to his groin.

'I haven't done any stitches since my time in med school,' she admitted, and swallowed.

The tension within him softened at her worried look, and he was filled with a different urge. He remembered the hurt in her voice when she'd told him about her time at the private practice she'd worked at. How she believed she'd compromised her career because of love.

A strange protectiveness wrapped itself around his chest. And, despite knowing that those feelings had no place within him, he wanted to be there for her. A foolish thought that he tried to brush aside.

'Doing stitches is like riding a bike. Once you start doing them again it will come back to you. Come,' he commanded, and he shook off the dark clouds gathering in his mind.

They left the supply cupboard and walked to the bed where Ms Scott was waiting.

'Lucy, this is my colleague, Dr Santos. Would you mind if she watched me do the sutures on your arm? We're a teaching hospital, and we want to give our doctors every opportunity to learn.'

Ms Scott nodded, and Mark took a seat on the stool next to the bed, indicating to Emma with the pointing of his finger to grab a chair from next to an empty bed and join him. As she sat down next to him the scent of coconut drifted up to his nose, and again he had to push the memories away. This patient deserved his undivided attention and, while his attraction to her made working with Emma a lot more complicated than he'd expected, she should still be able to learn from her senior surgeon. He'd told her he would teach her, and he meant to keep his promise.

Even though keeping his last promise of showing her Chicago had got him into hot water...

'Okay, this cut is clean and was inflicted by a sharp blade. That makes it a lot easier to stitch together. What is the challenge with uneven edges to a wound?'

Emma leaned in to look over his arm, a slight movement that brought an awareness of her to all his senses.

'Lining up the edges of the wound to close them is a lot less straightforward,' she said. 'If the edges are even, it will heal cleaner, leaving less scar tissue, and therefore is less likely to get inflamed.'

Mark nodded, wrestling his focus back to the patient in front of him. 'Exactly. So, first we'll put some local anaesthetic on, to make sure you'll be comfortable and still, as we do the stitches, Lucy.' He smiled at the patient to reassure her, and handed the anaesthetic cream that came with the suture kit to Emma. 'I don't need to explain that step to you,' he said, and she laughed at that, rolling her eyes before putting the cream on the patient's skin.

'What do you grow in your garden, Lucy?' Mark asked as they waited for the anaesthetic to numb the skin. If he could take her mind off the procedure for a moment, he would decrease her overall stress.

'All kinds of vegetables, but I'm most proud of my tomatoes this summer. Each year they're my worry child, with none of the plants coming in the way I want them to. But this year they did…' Her voice trailed off as she smiled, relaxing.

'They must be very popular in your neighbourhood. My late wife used to occupy herself with growing cucumbers. Everyone would get at least one jar of pickles from us.'

The memory had tumbled out of his mouth before he could stop himself. Talking about Claire had always been something he leaned on when connecting with a patient. The patient's needs always exceeded any discomfort he might feel at reawakening memories of her.

He didn't allow himself that kind of sentimentality around his staff, though. He wanted to be the rock they leaned on. But with Emma around, he found he didn't mind sharing those thoughts. Maybe they had become fond memories and he just hadn't realised it until he met her.

'Oh, no, you seem far too young to be a widower,' Ms Scott said.

Mark tried his best not to flinch at that. He never usually referred to Claire as his *late* wife, wanting to keep that detail to himself. How had that slipped out?

He turned his attention back to Emma. 'Since this cut is the best-case scenario, we can do simple sutures. Here, let me show you how to start.' He took the needle in between forceps and threaded it with the string from the kit. 'Lucy, you might want to look away for a moment,' he advised his patient, who raised her eyes to look at a TV at the far end of the room.

Mark aligned the edges of the wound and pulled the needle through one edge and then the other before pulling the string together and tying a precise but simple knot. He clipped the string close to the knot before threading the needle again and continuing in this fashion until only two stitches were left.

'I'm almost done here, Lucy. You're doing great. I will ask Dr Santos to do the last stitches under my supervision now, and then we'll bandage you up.'

Emma's head whipped around to him, her eyes wide in surprise. She opened her mouth, but he shook his head before she could protest.

'Take the forceps and the needle,' he said, passing her the tray of instruments before getting up to give her space to do the stitches.

He elected to stand, needing the extra space

between them to keep his mind focused. The soft scent of sweet coconut wrapped his head into a luscious fog of untold desire that he knew he must not get lost in.

He watched Emma pick up the instruments and follow his instructions. She placed two perfect stitches, and left no doubt in his mind that she remembered everything from her training. She didn't need any supervision from him, and it relieved him to see that. The less time he needed to spend with her in the free clinic, the better.

'All right, Lucy. Dr Santos will explain all the aftercare to you and send you on your way. Give your grandson a call so he can help,' he said, and took off his gloves, disposing of them in a bin nearby and then walking over to the counter to fill out some notes on the patient's chart.

He moved on to the next patient and saw from the corner of his eye that Emma had done the same. With both of them working on the stitches while the nurses kept on triaging the incoming patients, they had soon put a considerable dent in the number of people waiting to be treated.

As he finished up his latest set of notes Emma joined him at the admissions desk, a big smile gracing her face and lighting up the surrounding air.

'Thank you for taking the time to teach me,' she said as she reached him, leaving a deliberate few hand-spans of space between them. 'I was worried when Theresa asked me to come down here.'

Worried about what? How could she have known he'd be here?

'You came here to learn, and I promised I would teach you. That hasn't changed.' The words both of them left unspoken hung between them, recreating the tension sparking from her body to his and back. A spark that could cause a whole forest fire in mere seconds.

'I didn't see you on the OR board today. Are you not doing any surgery?' Emma asked, forcing his thoughts through the fog that was his awareness of her.

'It's my rest day today. I've exceeded the maximum hours I'm allowed to work in a week so the chief benched me.'

'Wait—you're here as a volunteer?'

'The chief doesn't like me spending my paid hours here, but there's more than enough work to go around so I come here whenever I can to help.'

Emma looked at him with such softness that his chest tightened and new sparks danced over his skin in a tantalising lure.

'That's so generous of you,' she said.

Her voice was only a whisper, and a light-ning bolt of desire struck his body as she smiled at him, robbing him of the ability to form any other thought than how to possess her.

A soft vibration interrupted him before he could reply, and Emma looked at her pager with a sigh. 'I have to check on some post-operative medication. I won't be long, if you still need my help.'

Mark lifted his hands to sweep them around him. 'We always need help down here, and we won't reject anyone willing to spend their time at the clinic.'

Emma nodded and then looked at him for a moment, as if expecting something, before turning around and running off to check up on her patient.

Mark let out a long sigh and took a few deep breaths, willing the fire coursing through his veins to ease so the heat within him would calm. There were patients waiting right at this moment while he was lusting after one of his subordi-nate physicians.

He shook his head to rid himself of any thought of Emma and grabbed the tablet, ready to work on the patients already admitted to the clinic. If he worked fast, and with no kind of distraction, he might be able to see everyone who'd come here for help today.

* * *

Emma's having to check up on one patient in the oncology department turned into several, along with answering a bunch of questions the interns had for her. By the time she got through all her tasks, her shift was over.

The sun had already set, and after grabbing her tote bag from her locker she made for the exit. Then she changed her mind at the last minute. Before leaving, she wanted to check on the free clinic. They must have closed by now, but if there were any patients still left to see, she wanted to ease the load.

Her heart stuttered inside her chest when her thoughts turned to Mark. There were at least five things she could list off the top of her head that she wanted to do on her days off. None of them involved leaving her house, and most of them were some form of sleeping. The long hours she worked at the hospital were tiring, leaving her like an empty husk most of the days.

Yet Mark went there on his day off, because he realised that the people who came needed help only a trained physician like himself could give.

The sheer kindness and generosity of such an act weakened Emma's knees. Something she was trying to avoid at all costs. Because that would add another layer to her attraction.

Another layer that made things so much more complicated.

She didn't want complicated. She wanted simple. Her move to Rochester was less than a month away now, and she was just learning to be by herself.

Her work in the oncology department was teaching her so much about the different conditions her patients presented, and how they coped with their diagnoses. It was strengthening her own resolve over her potential diagnosis. She wasn't ready to know yet, but she was determined to stick to her plan.

The way Mark spoke about his late wife had made her realise she couldn't let anyone get close to her until she'd figured her condition out for herself. By the sound of it, he and Claire had had their whole life planned out, only for her to be snatched away in an instant. Though while he now shared his memories of Claire more freely, Emma detected no hidden hurt underneath his words. After losing her mother, she'd thought the pain would never go away. It still hurt sometimes, often in the most innocent of moments, but those times became rarer as life went on.

The lights were still on when she approached the door of the free clinic, but as she entered she didn't see anyone at the admissions desk or in the patients' area. Had someone forgotten to turn off the lights?

As Emma walked around, looking for the light switch, she spotted Mark sitting at a table at the far end of the clinic, engrossed in whatever was in front of him. For a moment she hesitated, unsure whether she should approach him. Seeing him here had suddenly filled her with dread, and she was worried about what he might have to say about their kiss.

The kiss that had been lingering at the edge of her mind manifested itself fully, and for a brief moment his scent enveloped her once more. The memory caused a small spark in her stomach to reignite, sending warm showers in every direction of her body.

When agreeing to a tour of Chicago, Emma had not expected to kiss her boss. Or to have him reject her the way he had, with the sort of cool detachment she was used to seeing in other male surgeons.

The instant regret that had contorted his face still speared a sharp pain into her chest. His rejection had hurt more than she wanted to admit, even though the rational side of her brain should be rejoicing at the thought that she had extracted herself from a sticky situation with her senior surgeon. But Mark had set a chain of events in motion within her that he didn't even notice.

The more time she spent with him, the more she understood the diagnosis she had been avoiding since her mother passed away, and what kind of impact it might have on the people around her. She had convinced herself that she could wait until her training as a doctor was done. But what if she was wrong?

'Not even the free clinic lets you escape the paperwork,' she said, when she realised the patient charts were occupying his attention.

Mark looked up, clearly not having noticed her approach, and sighed. 'The clinic's is a lot harder. Since we treat a lot of uninsured people here, the board of directors at Alexander Attano wants to see where every single dollar goes.'

She took the seat next to him. 'So you're doing inventory more than patient notes?'

'Basically. Everything I use needs to be accounted for. You should see how much of a hassle it is when I need to account for my time.' He sighed and leaned back for a moment, scrubbing his hands over his face in a tired gesture. 'It's easier for me to come here on my days off rather than try to justify in front of the chief of surgery why I'm down here rather than in one of his ORs.'

Emma's chest tightened at the frustration visible in his stance. The free clinic obviously didn't get as much priority as he thought it should.

'Now that I know I can do that, I'll spend some time here,' she said, and her breath caught in her throat when Mark's gaze snapped to hers, his eyes darkening.

'You don't have to do that to please me,' he said.

She shook her head, sensing where his thoughts were headed. 'I'm not doing it to please anyone. I just want to help where I'm needed.' She shrugged when Mark raised an eyebrow at her. 'I'm only here for another month. I have nothing else going on, so I might as well do something meaningful with the time I have left.'

The way his eyes wandered down her entire body caused a shiver to trickle down her spine. All her senses were aware of his proximity.

'There's nothing else you would rather do for fun?' he asked after a brief period of quiet, his voice so low and full of gravel that it made her hair stand on end.

Was he flirting with her? After expressing regret about kissing her and before they had even found a moment to talk about their kiss?

'What I do for fun at the moment involves a lot of heavy medical textbooks,' she said, hoping the heat in her cheeks wasn't as visible as it felt. It was true. When she wasn't at the hospital, Emma put most of her time into studying for her fellowship. 'Though I've discovered that there's a greenhouse on the rooftop, which makes a pleasant change of scenery during my shifts. I don't have the greenest of thumbs, though I do find caring for plants soothing.'

'I'm in no position to reject any help that the free clinic gets offered, as long as you do it on your days off. Chief Singer would kill me if I started scheduling a very expensive locum tenens doctor into the clinic.'

Mark gave her a one-sided smile and for a moment they sat there in silence. Was each one of them trying to guess what the other was thinking? Should she say something? There wasn't that much to talk about on the surface. They'd kissed, he'd apologised for overstepping, and he'd left. Except that moment in the park hung between them, creating an air of strange closeness mixed with a significant amount of hesitation.

The sigh dropping from Mark's lips pulled her out of her contemplations. 'I'm not sorry I kissed you,' he said as he looked at her.

His smile had faded, leaving a veiled expression that Emma struggled to see through.

'It was inappropriate, as I'm the head of the department you work in. But I don't regret doing it.'

A surge of heat seized her body as she made sense of his words, her heart speeding up to a point where she could hear her blood rushing in her ears. Why was he saying that? His dark brown eyes were narrowed, intensifying the goosebumps already covering her flesh, and the spark in his gaze was reminiscent of what she had seen in the park right before he'd kissed her.

'I appreciate you saying that,' Emma said when she found her voice again, struggling to form the words with the big lump sitting in her throat.

She watched as he drew closer to her, her breath catching when his eyes flicked to her lips for a moment before coming back to her. Just like the last time when they had kissed. The ends of her nerves caught fire as she imagined kissing him again, and her entire body was aware of the minimal distance between them.

But Mark stopped with a wistful smile on his lips. He reached out with his hand, placing it on her cheek with unending gentleness. His thumb grazed over her cheekbone, with each sweep creating sparks that trickled down her body, raising the heat within her to new heights.

'I haven't been intimate with anyone since Claire passed away.'

The confession took Emma by surprise and she leaned back, her eyes wide. Even though he had shared some of his memories about Claire with her, it had never even occurred to her that he might not have been with anyone since her death. So the last person Mark had kissed before Emma had been his late wife…

Her mouth went dry as the thought manifested itself in her head, making it that much harder to swallow the still growing lump in her throat.

'Do you feel guilty about kissing another woman?' Emma asked.

She lacked any kind of reference point. The only person she knew who came close was her father, and he'd had no interest in dating after her mother passed away. Though she'd never asked him if it was because of guilt or other reasons. Did she want to hear that Mark felt he was betraying his late wife when he touched her?

But he shook his head. 'No, that's not what I feel guilty about.'

Then, ever so slowly, he leaned in. His nose touched hers first, grazing over the skin, and that minuscule touch was already enough to make her shiver with anticipation and need. She drew in a shaky breath and a firework exploded in the pit of her stomach, drowning out any thought when his lips touched hers.

She gave in to the sensation almost immediately, closing the tiny gap remaining between them. Infused by the fire his kiss sent licking across her skin, she opened her mouth to his, deepening their connection so she could feel it at her core, which contracted with each of his touches that elicited a response of untold desire.

He didn't feel guilty about being with another woman.

The meaning of those words was drowned out by the need surging through her. All she could focus on was where his hands were roaming over her body, making her writhe at every turn. Could she really be the first woman he'd been with after all these years? The moment seemed so monumental, so significant. How could she keep the emotional distance she needed to maintain?

Emma put her hands on his chest, forcing herself to break the intimate embrace. 'Wait…' She sighed, not sure what she wanted to say next.

Did she want to take things slowly? Despite her passionate reaction to his touch, she wasn't looking for another relationship. Mark fanned the flames of desire within her, making her react on impulse rather than following the plan she had set out. She couldn't afford to lose control or things would just end up like last time— for both of them.

Or was this the moment where she established the boundaries of what would be a casual affair? She had thought about the idea since arriving in Chicago, but had rejected it being with

Mark. If she dared to engage in something with no strings attached it couldn't be with her superior. Or did those things not matter in affairs?

Mark let go of her, and the space he created between them felt like an insurmountable chasm that filled her with instant regret. The longing for his touch rushed to the forefront of her mind, tempting her to disregard her caution. She tried reading his expression, wondering if his blood was running just as hot as hers. The fire in his eyes caused her breath to catch in her throat, but behind that she spotted something else mingling with the desire written on his face.

Was he not sure if he was ready for something, either?

'I think we should talk about this first,' she said, with a slight shake in her voice.

Mark cleared his throat before he nodded and started to respond. Yet the words he meant to speak never crossed his lips. A shrill beeping coming from Emma's bag interrupted him.

'Are you *serious* right now?' she said under her breath, digging through her bag to find her pager just as Mark's pager beeped with the same urgency. Was there no moment when they could talk without being interrupted by some kind of emergency?

He grabbed his pager with a frown and jumped to his feet as he read the message. '911 page for Georgina,' he said, and Emma's pulse quickened.

They hurried to the oncology department where Georgina had begun chemotherapy after her tumour had been found to be malignant. They found two interns in the room, doing chest compressions to resuscitate their patient. Emma went over to her monitor, checking her vitals. Mark barked orders as a nurse wheeled the crash cart into the room to administer the medicine he'd ordered.

'Her blood pressure is coming back up,' Emma said as the epinephrine kicked in, and she let out a sigh of relief when Georgina's pulse evened out and steadied itself. 'How did this happen? I know she's struggled with the side effects of her chemo, but it shouldn't cause heart failure. Apparently earlier this morning she was sitting up gossiping with the nurses.'

Mark walked out of the patient's room to the nurses' station, where he took a tablet to check out the latest scans. A different tension built around them now as Emma stood next to him, watching as he scrutinised the images on the tablet.

After a long stretch of silence he pointed at the part of the scan that showed Georgina's thyroid. Emma stared at it before lifting her eyebrows. 'It looks clean to me. And the biopsy of the lymph node came back inconclusive.'

'I don't think it is. Call it a hunch.'

He waved an intern over, instructing him to do more scans once Georgina was stable enough, and asking if Harald was still here. When the intern nodded, Mark sighed. The toll this day was taking on him was visible in the deep lines on his face.

'I can talk to him,' Emma offered, wanting to lessen his burden in any way she could.

But he shook his head. 'I'll update him and then head out. Georgina will need to recover before she can be moved to the CT. We'll be able to go over the scans tomorrow morning.'

Emma nodded, feeling her stomach tying itself into a knot as she watched him walk away. It was as if a gloomy presence had taken hold of him as he'd looked at Georgina's scans, and it was filling Emma's chest with worry. The urge to look after him pulsed through her, and she caught up with the intern Mark had just spoken to.

'Page me when the scans are up,' she said, thinking the chances were that Mark would wait around to gain some clarity about their patient.

'We'll do more tests once she's stable.'

Mark placed his hand on Harald's shoulder

as the man digested all the information he had just given him about his wife's condition.

'This is not all bad news. She's alive, and we'll have a deeper look at the cause of her heart failure.'

Harald looked like a husk of a man, his eyes unfocused. The sight wrenched at his heart, reminding him of when he had been in Harald's place. Georgina's case reminded him so much of Claire and his own experience that he felt the wounds of his past tearing open under the pressure.

Mark knew he should distance himself…not get too attached to the fate of a patient. But each time he looked at Harald he saw himself in his shoes, and he was fighting hard to prevent him from having to deal with the pain of losing his wife.

He walked to his office rather than to his car to go home. It would take a couple of hours for Georgina's condition to be stable enough to move her. Enough time for him to stretch out on the couch in his office to see if he could fall asleep.

He dropped down on the soft cushions, closing his eyes for just a moment before a faint knock drifted to his ear. 'Enter,' he said, too consumed by his own thoughts to get off his seat.

To his surprise, Emma came in, balancing

two takeaway coffee cups on top of one another while closing the door with her other hand.

She hesitated before she smiled. 'I came here to convince you to go home for the evening, but in case that didn't work I brought some coffee to keep you going.' She looked around for a moment. 'You don't actually have an apartment, you live here—am I right?'

Her quip pierced through the fog enveloping him and a genuine chuckle crossed his lips. 'Don't tell anyone. They'll revoke my privileges.'

Emma touched her lips in a gesture as if she was zipping them closed before stepping towards him and handing him a cup. 'I'm heading home. See you tomorrow.'

'Wait.' Mark looked out of the window, noticing how much time had passed since they'd left the clinic. 'Let me walk you to your car. It's dark outside, and I know how far away they make the temporary staff park.'

'That's unnecessary,' Emma said with a deflecting smile, but he was already on his feet and opening the door for her to escort her through the car park.

He had to admit that he was doing it for himself as much as for her. When he was near her, the shadows surrounding him didn't feel as oppressive, and at this moment he needed that. He couldn't let her go just yet.

When she'd come to find him in the clinic, he'd had no intention of sharing so much of his feelings, despite them being true. The thought of being close to another woman frightened him to some extent, but Emma evoked something within him he hadn't felt in ages, and before he'd been able to stop himself his lips had already been moving, sharing his thoughts with her.

His mind struggled to grapple with what that meant, and he didn't want to think about it. For once he just wanted to feel as if things might be okay one day.

'Are you kidding me?'

Emma sighed when they got closer to her car, and he watched her kneel behind one of her rear tyres. It was flat.

He reached out his hand to help her up and a hot spark travelled down his arm when her delicate fingers wrapped themselves around his hand. Their hands remained intertwined for a moment before she withdrew, leaving him aware of the space between them.

'Come on, I'll drive you home,' he said, but she shook her head.

'Thank you, but that's unnecessary. I'll take a cab and call a tow truck in the morning.'

She started when he grabbed her hand again and walked her to his parking spot.

'Don't be silly. I'll drive you home now and you can take a cab in the morning, as a compromise. How does that sound?'

He refused to heed any more protests, and surprised himself when he found the way to her flat without having to consult the navigation system. Somehow once had been enough for him to remember.

Mark pulled up in front of her building and turned to her to say something, but the words died in his throat when his gaze met hers. There was an intensity brimming in the dark green eyes that drew him to her like tiny insects to a roaring flame.

'Do you want to come up?' she said, and Mark narrowed his eyes for a moment.

'What?'

'I mean to talk about the case. I found some takeout menus in a drawer, so we could order some food while we strategize. You've had a long day—maybe a second set of eyes might be helpful.'

Of course that was it. How could his mind have even thought of anything else? And the answer was no. He didn't want to go up. Except he did. Desperately. The darkness closing in on him lifted the moment Emma came close, and today the fog was more suffocating than usual.

Even though he knew that at some point he would have to surrender himself to the encroaching darkness again, just for a few hours he wanted to escape.

'Sure, let's work out how we can help Georgina,' he said with a nod, and followed her up the stairs.

CHAPTER EIGHT

EMMA'S HAND SHOOK as she put the key into her apartment door, opening it up and inviting Mark in. Why had she done that? The second the invitation had left her lips she'd wanted to snatch it back and swallow it whole.

Ever since her second day at Attano Memorial, when she had almost kissed him in the on-call room, Emma had failed at keeping her distance. To invite him up to her apartment now was the cherry on top of the sundae that was her awful decision-making.

It was about food and helping Georgina, Emma told herself. The way he'd looked at her when she'd entered his office had made her heart ache with sympathy. The defeat in his eyes had been palpable.

Mark looked around him and wandered over to her living room, leaving her alone with the takeout menus. A few medical journals and textbooks were stacked on top of the coffee table. He plopped down on the couch, browsing through the journals and then grabbing one, flipping it open at random. To keep herself from staring at him, she took out the paper pamphlets from the drawer.

'Do we want late-night burgers, or just a gigantic pizza?' she asked.

There was no reply. Then, 'I haven't seen this one in ages.'

His voice trailed off and Emma looked up from the stack of menus. What had fascinated him so much that he couldn't answer the important question of food?

The second she heard him laugh she understood which journal he had found and rushed over, throwing herself on the couch to take it away from him. 'You were not supposed to see that!'

Mark moved the hand holding the magazine above his head and out of her reach and she climbed on top of him to pull the journal out of his grip. She stretched her arm, her fingertips unable to reach their goal.

'Dr Handsome?' he asked, with amusement shining in his eyes.

Her habit of writing her thoughts and feelings in the margins of the magazine was coming back to haunt her. The man who'd written the article had just read her thoughts about *him*.

Her hand was resting on his broad chest, their faces only inches apart. It was then that she realised how close she had got to him to take the medical journal away from him. Fire rose to her cheeks, leaving a burning trail throughout her body as she commanded her brain to put some distance between them. But her body did not heed her. All she could focus on was his warm breath grazing the already hot skin of her face.

Her entire being trembled when Mark dropped the journal on the floor so his fingers could touch her cheek. He cocked his head, his dark eyes entrancing her as a snake charmer would enthral his pet reptile to do his bidding.

A small smile appeared on his lips. 'I didn't know you liked me *that* much,' he said teasingly, driving a spear of hot lava into her centre.

'I don't,' she lied. But her voice failed her on those important two words. If there ever was a time to sound sure of herself it was now, and yet her lower lip quivered as she drew in a shaky breath.

'Then how come you kissed me twice?'

'Me? You were the one kissing me—both times.' The words sounded a lot more defensive than she'd meant them to be.

'I don't know… That doesn't sound like something I'd do. Let me try to jog my memory.' His playful tone quickened her pulse. She watched as his face closed in on hers, and a moment later he'd captured her mouth in an earth-shattering kiss.

Everything around Emma faded away as she lost herself in Mark's touch. More demanding this time around, he pulled her against him, his hands finding the seams of her clothing and pushing the top over her head in an almost frantic motion.

This moment had been a long time coming, and neither wanted to wait another second. Her thoughts went to their kiss in the clinic. She had stopped him then, wanting to talk about this attraction between them. Emma liked clear rules and boundaries within which she could operate. But how had the rules helped her in her last relationship? Even when she had done everything the way she was supposed to, supporting Rob and putting his needs ahead of hers?

Emma was done with letting her past experience dictate to her. She had left and it was time to be brave, to embrace the moment. They were both here, both willing. What else was there to know?

This kiss was nothing like the tender moments they'd shared earlier. Their desire and need was setting both of them alight to the point where the fulfilment of their passion for each other was the only thing dominating their thoughts. This was what she wanted in this moment. They'd have plenty of time to talk about it later.

Throwing the piece of fabric on the floor, Mark dipped his head, trailing kisses along her collarbone. His tongue licked around the hollow of her neck before finding his way down her sternum.

She shivered when he pushed her bra aside, releasing the stiff peaks of her nipples that had already been straining against the silk of her underwear. A moan dropped from her lips when his warm breath grazed her breast before he took her dark nipple into his mouth, lavishing her sensitive skin with the untold pleasure she had seen written in his eyes since their encounter in the park.

What did she have to lose? Neither of them was looking for something serious. This was her moment to relinquish control and to learn how to go with the flow. To 'let loose', as she'd been told.

Her hands wandered down his back, feeling the hardness of his broad shoulders as she looked for something to hold on to. To anchor her in this world as the fire of passion within her immolated everything in its wake. She tore at his clothes with unprecedented urgency. A growl left his throat when she pushed him away from her to yank the scrub top off his body.

The wetness of her core caused a shiver to cascade through her body as she drank in the view of his bare chest. Her eyes wandered down, following the line of hair as it vanished below his waistband. Her gaze drifted further, and her breath caught in her throat when she saw his erect manhood straining against the fabric of his trousers.

She reached out, biting her lower lip as she did so, but his hand closed around her wrist. He stopped her before she got to fulfil all her fantasies of the past couple of weeks. And then he smiled at her, and all her walls and insecurities came tumbling down at that pure expression of affection. It stoked the fire within her into a frenzy she'd never experienced before in her life.

'Bedroom?' he asked, and Emma pointed down the corridor to the single door standing ajar.

As she tried to get up, he wrapped his hands around her waist and picked her up. She yelped at her sudden loss of footing and wrapped her legs around his hips to help her balance while her arms encircled his neck.

He nuzzled his face into her neck, making fire lick over her skin as he walked them to the bedroom. He dropped her on her bed with surprising gentleness. As he straightened himself he hooked his fingers into her trousers, dragging them down and throwing them behind him before pouncing back on top of her.

Emma writhed under the look Mark gave her as his eyes drank her in, passing over her ample curves with unveiled hunger and longing. Then his mouth found hers again and fireworks exploded all around Emma's body as their bare skin touched, the sensation overwhelming her. And just as she thought she couldn't feel any more bliss than he'd already given her, his hand slipped past the silken fabric of her underwear and his deft fingers found her sensitive spot.

A bolt of lightning shook her entire body, meeting the waves of pleasure crashing through her and creating a perfect storm at her core, blurring the fine line between pleasure and pain. She gasped, a part of her wanting to retreat from this exquisiteness. But the part within her that had hungered for Mark the second she'd laid eyes on him was much stronger.

She was ready to get lost in this moment. With this man.

Emma moaned against his lips as his talented fingers coaxed her over the cliff, shattering her into a million pieces. Her head tilted backwards, and all of her instincts were occupied with keeping her mind intact enough to kiss him back.

For a longing moment Emma thought this must be the end. There could be nothing else to give. Yet Mark was determined to prove her wrong. His mouth trailed along her neck while his hand let go of her to relieve her of her underwear, tossing it aside. The feral look in his eyes caused a shiver to claw through her body as she prepared for what was about to happen.

Mark laughed when he caught her gaze trailing downwards, to where his manhood was still contained by his trousers. 'You *do* like me,' he said with a grin.

'No, I don't,' she replied in defiance, though her hands betrayed her words as they wandered over his broad chest and down his abdomen, appreciating the hard ridges of his muscles for a moment before slipping under his trousers. Her heart beat against her chest as she wrapped her hand around him and heard a muffled groan escape his lips. 'In fact, I think you're the one who likes me.'

Mark chuckled again, a playful gleam in his eyes as he stood up to peel himself out of his remaining clothes, standing in front of her in all his glory. 'Preposterous! You have no evidence to support such a claim.'

Instead of saying anything Emma grinned,

her eyes moving to his erection before coming back to his face. She raised an eyebrow in a silent question.

'We're both doctors. You should know that this results from external stimuli and not emotion,' he said.

And before she could say anything else he was on her again, his mouth capturing hers, pulling her into the sheets with a kiss charged with the sexual tension that had been building up since they'd first met.

'Speaking of being responsible doctors…' His voice trailed off for a moment, as if he was looking for the right words.

'I have an IUD,' she said, understanding what he was about to ask.

'That doesn't help with all the other risky things.'

Emma paused for a moment as the heat from her core shot up to her cheeks. 'I've rarely done this kind of thing. And definitely not recently.'

The smile that appeared on his lips took the breath out of her lungs. He lowered his face to kiss along her neck again, coming to a brief stop next to her ear. 'Good. Neither do I,' he whispered, before his mouth found hers again.

Emma opened her lips to him, felt their tongues creating an erotic dance that threatened to undo her all over again. She would be his first woman since the death of his wife. The thought got through the luscious fog enveloping them. But did it even matter? He was a willing participant, just as she was. It didn't need to mean anything—and who was she to decide that this needed to be an important moment for him?

Her body trembled, aching for his touch, and Emma let go of the last remaining shreds of control she was hanging on to. Her legs fell open as he positioned himself between them, and the desire to have him controlled every single thought in her mind. She held her breath as his length pressed against the apex of her thighs, and a moment later she felt whole.

Emma wrapped her arms around his neck as he rocked against her, their lips connecting again as he thrust into her with a certainty that sent sparks flying all over her skin. The primal groans coming from his throat with every thrust filled her belly with wild butterflies. Knowing that she'd brought a man this kind of intense pleasure threatened to undo her both body and mind.

He wanted her just as much as she wanted him.

She hung on to his back, her hands digging into his flesh as the sweet fingers of her next climax clawed at her, and as if reading her mind Mark slipped his hand between them to caress her, sending lightning bolts through all her extremities.

Emma sobbed his name as she fell apart in his arms, letting herself get lost in the pleasure of their lovemaking. She pulled his face to her lips in a last kiss as Mark shuddered above her with a guttural growl before collapsing on top of her.

The smell of food broke through the heavy blanket of sleep surrounding Emma, and with a start she sat up. The space next to her was empty. Her mouth went dry as memories of last night came rushing back into her consciousness, reigniting the fire that had kept her going for the last hours.

Had he left?

The tension in her chest only lasted a second, dispersing as she walked out of the bedroom and caught a glance of Mark standing in front of the stove, wearing nothing but his underwear.

The sight of his lithe and muscular body, of him standing in her kitchen, made her knees weak as a myriad of different emotions started a fight for dominance within her. The wetness that the sight of him brought to her core showed her that their night together had done precious little to satiate her growing hunger for the man in front of her.

Her boss.

The thought dropped a heavy boulder into the pit of her stomach. Last time she'd let herself fall for her boss the relationship had turned into a toxic mess that she'd only just untangled herself from.

Except this wasn't a relationship. They'd had sex one time. She didn't want a relationship anyway, she reminded herself. Not with her leaving Chicago soon.

Despite their brief acquaintance with each other, Emma felt she had got to know Mark over the last couple of weeks. He'd shared so much about his life in Rochester with her, letting her know about the good and the bad things surrounding his previous marriage. How much it shaped him to this day.

Another reason not to get attached.

What if Emma fell ill with the same disease that had taken her mother? The chances were there, however unlikely, and she had yet to get tested for it. Mark would never want to involve himself with a cancer diagnosis waiting to happen.

'I don't know why it surprises me to see you cooking, but it's not something I ever imagined for you,' Emma said as she approached the counter, trying to quell the storm brewing inside her. Every fibre of her begged to jump back into his arms. Every inch of distance between their bodies sizzled on her skin like a hot iron, intensifying the ache in her core.

'As a physician, you should understand how important a balanced diet is,' he said with a smirk, as he opened a few cupboards until he found the plates. 'I used to do most of the cooking even before Claire got too sick to do it. We worked the same hours at the clinic, but she was way more driven than I was.'

Claire. The name suddenly rang with a familiarity that she hadn't sensed before. She and Mark had worked together at the Whitebridge Institute before she'd got sick. How come Emma had never heard of her if she'd been so closely linked to his work?

Then she remembered where she'd read the name before, and her jaw fell open. 'Wait—your wife was Dr Claire Dubois? Your co-author?'

Emma's gaze moved over her shoulder to look at the stack of medical journals on her coffee table.

Mark looked up from the pan, a slight smile softening the lines around his mouth. 'That's her. She was an anaesthesiologist as well—though when we worked together she only focused on our research around pain management.' He paused for a moment and chuckled. 'She did most of the writing—she was much better at putting our findings into words.'

Emma raised her eyebrows in surprise. Unfamiliar feelings bubbled up inside her stomach as she considered his words. The last thing she'd expected to hear this morning were more fond memories of his wife. It didn't bother her, but it intrigued her. Had he reached the point where he was ready to move on from his marriage?

Though another part of his sentence also stood out to Emma. 'Claire wrote all the papers?'

Mark nodded with a one-sided smile. 'I don't think people understood my ramblings and tangents.'

The realisation stunned Emma. 'I can't believe it. All this time I thought it was you, when in actuality I fell in love with the words of your wife.'

The dreaded word had crossed her lips before she could stop herself. Emma cringed, instant regret wiping out all other emotions dancing in her chest. Why had she said the L-word when any other word would have done?

'She was an excellent writer,' Mark said, and nothing in his face betrayed whether he'd taken exception to her words or if he even cared. Instead, he focused on the task in front of him, finishing up their breakfast as he spoke. 'Maybe that was one reason why I stepped away from research. I love the discovery and the progress, but I never enjoyed writing. That task belonged to her, and I guess I wasn't ready to let someone else take over a part of the research that was so important to her.'

'Do you feel ready for it now?'

Emboldened by his previous words, she asked the question. Mark had just shared a side of him she hadn't known about. Despite her putting her foot in her mouth a mere few seconds ago, she decided to push on. They had just spent a night of toe-curling passion with each other, and while Emma still guarded herself, she wanted to peep behind the curtains.

He looked at her, his expression letting her know he hadn't missed the subtext in her words. Being ready to let someone else step into his life applied to more aspects than just his research work.

Mark sat down on the barstool next to her, his eyes glued to the plate in front of him for a moment. 'I don't know. I've never had time to think about it.' He stopped for a moment, contemplating. 'The head of research at the institute has been courting me ever since I left. They seem to miss me there.'

'Would you ever go back?' Emma tried to sound casual, as if the answer didn't matter to her. It shouldn't, anyway, because entertaining any thoughts of both of them living in the same city long term was ridiculous. It implied an emotional connection where there couldn't be one.

Her heart twinged inside her chest when Mark shook her head with a resolute finality. 'I can't go back to that place—not for anything. It's where I lost everything that's ever been important to me.'

His voice came out in a strange monotone, and an instant later she saw those walls come up in front of his eyes. He looked at her, but his expression was guarded, not letting her see the exact effect those memories were having on him.

Strange thoughts were chasing each other in Emma's mind—thoughts she tried to stop. His answer shouldn't mean anything to her. She didn't want him to come to Rochester with her because she didn't want a relationship with him. So his answer shouldn't hurt the way it did.

'Even for someone on the go, four cardboard boxes seem like very little to fit your entire life into,' he said, changing the subject as they finished their breakfast. He was looking around the bare apartment with a strange expression.

An embarrassed heat shot into her cheeks as she followed his eyes. 'I left the city in somewhat of a hurry and only took the things that were important to me.' She stopped for a moment, considering her next words. 'I wanted a fresh start.'

His gaze narrowed on her. 'What did he do to you?' he asked, and Emma wasn't sure how to answer the question.

The hurt caused by Rob was something that still haunted her, even though he was miles away and had no more power over her now than she was willing to give him. The comparison between her failed relationship and her current entanglement was easy to make, but did it mean it was true? Mark was so different from her ex-boyfriend and he had shown her that ten times over. Maybe trusting him would be okay—as long as they remained clear that this was only a casual affair.

It wouldn't hurt her. She would make sure she wouldn't fall. She would not let anyone get close to her until she'd answered the question about her potential Gardner's diagnosis. No matter how different Mark was.

'He convinced me to give up my spot at the hospital to work under him at his private practice. I was worried that my training wouldn't be as well-rounded as I needed it to be. But he brushed these concerns aside, insisting on his need to develop his career as a plastic surgeon. He promised me that once he'd made a name for himself it would be my turn. When I told him they'd accepted me into a programme at the Whitebridge Institute that promise meant precious little. He refused to leave, trying to convince me that I would be better off as his staff anaesthesiologist and to give up my fellowship. When I wouldn't, he tried to discredit me in front of our contacts in the medical community. He couldn't cope with the fact that he had lost control over me.'

She paused for a moment, the memory of many abusive messages and late-night knocks on her door flooding back into her consciousness. Despite her best efforts to forget everything about Rob and his treatment of her, tears stung her eyes, and she blinked them away.

This wasn't a part of her life Emma had planned on sharing with anyone, and yet here she was, baring her soul to Mark right after they'd spent the night together. For a fleeting moment, she wondered what he would think if she told her that she might be sick, too. She had tried to reveal her secret to Rob, but her attempts had fallen on deaf ears. His main concern over her condition was whether or not it would impact on her work.

Would Mark feel deceived and lied to if she told him? Was she even obligated to talk to him about it?

The shame of her own shortcomings as a doctor burned in her chest and she hardly dared to look at him, too scared to see judgement in his expression. But his eyes were not chastising or demeaning. They shone with kindness. And something else hiding beneath. An unbridled fury.

In one fluid motion he got to his feet and pulled her from her seat to crush her against his chest. He dipped his head to capture her mouth with his, wiping all thought from her brain.

'You are a powerful woman of amazing calibre. He is the villain in this story. You aren't to blame for believing his words were sincere when they weren't.'

He held her close, his low voice vibrating through her as she wrapped her arms around him, feeling again the sting of tears in her eyes.

'Believing the person you love is as natural as breathing. Don't blame yourself.'

Emma had been terrified of being judged. Yet Mark cradled her with affection, his hands stroking her back as she worked through the pain.

They remained like that for a moment, with her head lying against her chest. Then Mark's hands drifted from her back up to her neck, cupping each side of her face as he drew her into a gentle kiss.

'Look, I don't want things to be awkward between us,' he said when their lips had parted, his voice a low growl that vibrated all the way to her bones. 'You are an amazing woman of stunning beauty and I admire your skill as a doctor. I've told you how I haven't been in any kind of relationship outside of marriage, and I don't think I'm ready for anything serious. I don't know if I ever will be.'

'It doesn't have to be serious,' she replied in a whisper, convincing herself that this was the truth. The fact that she had just shared her past hurt with him didn't change the fact that she wasn't looking for love. It didn't matter that her heart beat against her chest, longing for the gentle kindness she had just seen in his eyes. 'I'm leaving in a matter of weeks. We can leave it at that. A clean cut.'

Emma knew they couldn't have more. Not when she might slip away at any moment, tumbling down the same path as her mother. The threat of her own condition dangled over her head, ever-present.

His firm hand became more demanding. He slipped it under her shirt as he pressed her against him, first caressing her back, before slipping to her front, cupping her breast in his palm as his thumb brushed over her reaching nipple. Her mind and body wrapped in the sensual cloud produced by Mark's touch and proximity, Emma took a deep breath in a futile effort to calm the storm raging within her.

All her thoughts were drawn to the present moment when Mark's hand slipped to her back again, crushing her against him as he deepened the kiss. His full length pressed against the apex of her thighs, his hunger as ravenous as it had been last night. Her hands wandered down his spine, and nimble fingers found the edge of his underwear. It fell to the floor with a single tug, drawing a growl from Mark's throat.

Emma gasped when he grabbed her by the waist and picked her up. She wrapped her legs around his midsection, and as she found her balance his tip found her entrance.

'Bedroom?' she asked between mewls, as his head dipped down to her breasts to lick and suck at her dark nipples.

'Right here,' he replied, with an imposing certainty that brought a shiver down to her core.

'Right here is good,' she said.

And she gasped again when Mark took two steps so that her back leaned against the cold wall behind her. His hands cupped her buttocks as he angled himself, and a skipped heartbeat later her thighs trembled as he plunged into her.

CHAPTER NINE

THE FOG AROUND Mark had lifted, and for the first time in ages he could breathe again. Not only could he live again, he could enjoy the company of a woman without having the soul-crushing weight of guilt sitting on his chest every step of the way. For that, he was grateful, and it was that feeling that made him want to spend himself with Emma over and over again.

Each night of the last week they'd ended up in Emma's apartment, arms and legs and hair intertwined until exhaustion took them. But he was worried about things getting messy.

Her confession of what had driven her to leave San Francisco left him in a state of perpetual fury each time he remembered how she'd been mistreated and discarded. To think someone had been cruel enough to waste her affection in such a manner brought Mark's blood to a boil.

So much so, he had to remind himself to stay

grounded. The physical passion they shared ran so hot he needed to rein himself in. Despite how brilliant she was, he needed to be careful not to let his emotions stray. He was not at liberty to promise his heart to anyone, and he needed to stay within the boundaries they'd agreed on.

His broken self would never be enough for her.

Mark's gaze wandered over her now, and hunger was stirring in his chest when the soft buzz of his phone interrupted his lustful plans. Peeling his eyes away from her, he checked his messages and frowned.

'The oncologist has cleared Georgina for further treatment.'

Emma, curled up in his arms on the couch beside him, looked up with a furrowed brow. 'It took her a long time to stabilise after the strain of chemotherapy,' she said, giving voice to his thoughts. 'Can you ask them to send over the updated scans? We can look at them once they arrive.'

Georgina's recovery from her heart failure a week ago had been a slow and arduous process that troubled Mark more than he wanted to admit. So much about her case revived the memories he had buried alongside his wife.

Emma interrupted his contemplations when she wound herself out of his grasp to look through the journals and textbooks piled onto the coffee table.

'I remember reading about a case just like that…' she said.

'I don't think this is a medical mystery. I see it all the time in oncology. There was only a hint of metastasis on the scan before, too small for the naked eye. It will probably be visible on the scans now.'

He watched her with a small smile on his lips as she leafed through a journal. As he traced her voluptuous curves with his hands a fire ignited in his groin when she glanced over her shoulder with a suggestive wink, before putting her attention back on the journal in her hands.

Even a slight gesture like that was enough to reawaken the searing passion within him. Emma had found a way around the daunting defences he'd built and nestled herself into a warm spot. She'd even got him to talk about his late wife without the oppressive darkness consuming him. In her presence he found himself free to appreciate his memories for what they were.

There was no way Mark would ever let himself love again. But he could be happy with a temporary affair. Emma was leaving in a matter of days, which would end their dalliance as painlessly as possible. There would be no misunderstandings about emotional attachment or love.

His eyes drifted away from the deliciousness that was her body to the different books lying around. Quite a few of them were textbooks specifically around oncology, with bookmarks sticking out of them to mark specific passages.

He opened the first book at a marker and inspected the passage. It was in-depth diagnostical research around Gardner Syndrome. Mark closed his eyes for a moment, recalling what he knew about the disease. His search for a cure, or even just an edge to help Claire survive longer, had put him in front of a lot of different types of cancer. He wasn't an expert in genealogy, but looking at what made certain conditions hereditary helped him understand the disease on a more fundamental level.

To his surprise, the next book had passages concerning genetic cancer diseases like Gardner Syndrome marked as well. 'What's your interest in Gardner's?' he asked, and watched as she paled. His chest constricted as a harrowing thought entered his mind. She wouldn't have kept that kind of information from him, right? 'Do you...?' His voice trailed off, and he sighed with relief when she shook her head.

But the silence enveloping them now was deafening as he watched a myriad of different expressions flutter over her face. Her chest rose and fell, becoming more pronounced as she put the journal down. She hesitated for a moment, licking her lips, and took a deep breath before she spoke.

'No, I don't think so.'

The relief washing over him was warped again as he interpreted her words. 'You don't *think* so? Do you have any family history?'

Emma swallowed visibly, her eyes darting around for a moment before looking at him again. There was another pregnant pause, as if she had to think about her answer. Was there some obscure relative who had once shown signs of the disease?

'My mother had Gardner Syndrome.'

Her *mother*? Gardner Syndrome could be passed on from parent to child. If a child had the genetic marker for the disease, part of the early prevention system was to get regular cancer screenings, so any potential tumours could be caught early. Why had she not mentioned it?

'When was your last scan?' he asked.

She squirmed under his knowing look.

A foreboding sense of dread settled in Mark's chest when Emma remained quiet, avoiding his probing gaze. Tension wound itself into a coil in his abdomen as he awaited her answer. He suddenly found himself in a situation so familiar that he felt the same naked fear creep out of the corners of his memories.

'I've had a prophylactic scan before my internship ended. But no official diagnosis.'

Mark swore under his breath and got up from the couch as hot fury replaced the chilling dread in his veins. 'Get dressed. We're going to the hospital right now,' he said, and picked up his clothing from where he had dropped it the night before.

'Mark, this isn't your problem,' Emma said, pushing her chin out with a defiant gaze.

'You are a doctor, Emma. Someone who works with cancer patients day in and day out. You know better than anyone what this disease can do to people, and yet you have not tried to ensure your own health is cared for when you know you might have a genetic condition.' He balled his hands into fists at her dismissive look. 'Have you even done the genetic test?'

Emma shook her head. 'My father urged me to get tested, but I don't want to. At least not yet…' She left the rest of the sentence unspoken.

Mark stared at her. He felt an icy hand gripping his insides as he came to understand the full gravity of the situation. Despite working with cancer patients every day, Emma hadn't looked after her own health and had ignored the potential diagnosis of a disease that could change her life in the worst possible way. How could she not have acted on this information? Did the people in her life mean so little to her? Did he?

'Why not? You have first-hand knowledge of what kind of situation this can be. Why would you not prepare yourself?'

'It's because of *this*, right here, that I didn't want to know. Now to you I'm Emma, potential Gardner Syndrome patient, rather than your...' Her voice choked and fear entered her eyes.

The tension within him dissolved when he caught that frightened look. Relaxing his hands and taking a deep breath, he forced himself to remain calm. The terror in her eyes had struck at his heart, and the twinging inside his chest was great concern for her.

Though that concern was almost overwritten by immediate detachment as his mind shifted into doctor mode and sought to create some distance between him and the situation. It was the same pattern of behaviour that had made him miss those last days with Claire. That wasn't the man he wanted to be.

He forced a couple of breaths into his lungs, reminding himself of the fear Claire's sudden revelation had struck in his heart. The same was true for Emma—only amplified by several magnitudes. And if he was scared in this moment, she must be terrified.

Could he be there for her the way he hadn't been able to be present for Claire? It wouldn't make up for his past failings, but maybe he would be able to reclaim something of the person he'd used to be.

Mark sat back down, putting his hand under her chin and lifting it so she would look at him.

'I never took the test because I've never felt ready to know,' she said. 'If I know I have the gene mutation I'll have to plan. I'll have to… make peace.'

Her voice faltered and tears fell down her cheeks. He wiped them away with his thumbs before pulling Emma into his arms.

'You don't have to get tested if you aren't ready. But we should get you a scan at the very least. You know how much early intervention can help with a prognosis.'

Emma buried her face in his shoulder for a moment, before nodding.

'We'll get you in for some blood work, a CT and an MRI scan, so dress accordingly,' he said, before releasing her and putting on his own clothes.

It had been a few years since Emma had seen the inside of a CT machine. The last time had been just before her internship had ended. After learning about her mother's diagnosis, Gardner Syndrome had become a constant companion in her life. A source of chaos when she wanted control. Especially as Emma had got used to driving her destiny forward, pursuing her goals in her own way.

A terminal illness did not fit in with that plan, and she hadn't known how to control the chaos it had brought into her life. So she'd done what she knew best: she'd made a plan. It hadn't ben a good plan, she had to admit. But it had given her something to hang on to. Her life would move along the path she had planned until her fellowship ended, and then she would have time to cope with anything else.

Now, Mark's words kept replaying in her head—but, more than that, his experience as a surviving spouse of a cancer victim struck a terrifying chord within her.

Had she let things go too far? Their connection was explosive, their passion for each other infusing her mind and body alike. But the hurt in his face when she'd told him about her family history with Gardner's had taken her breath away. He'd seemed genuinely concerned about her wellbeing. And what that meant terrified her. Such concern didn't mix well with the casual nature of their affair. Was this another part of her life where she had lost control?

He had shared his struggles with her, let her see the uncensored pain that he kept hidden from anyone else. He'd trusted her, and that solidified her resolve. She couldn't permit herself to feel this surge of emotion bubbling beneath the surface of their casual entanglement. For her sake as much as his.

'We're almost done. Hang in there for a couple more moments.'

As if her thoughts had summoned him, Mark's voice came through the speakers of the machine, mixing the dread dwelling within her with something else that she wanted to focus on even less.

Emma pushed thoughts of him away as a shiver brought on by memories of his unreserved concern for her threatened to rock her body. His anger had scared her almost as much as her potential diagnosis. But behind it she'd glimpsed the true nature of his fury—a deep affection for her. It was a thought that scared her all over again. What if he wanted something from her that she couldn't give him?

The machine rattled and hummed around her and she closed her eyes to block out all thought. A moment later the noise stopped, and she was pulled out of the machine.

Mark waved her into a booth where her scans were already on a screen. Her gait was unsteady as nervousness flooded her system, and as much as she willed her head to turn, to inspect the scans, her eyes remained on Mark, watching his face for some kind of sign.

Relief washed away the dreadful uncertainty coiling in the pit of her stomach when he gave her a small smile accompanied by a nod. 'We're still going to do some blood work, but the scans look clean.'

Emma released her breath, only just noticing that she had been holding it all this time. 'That's good news.' With a sigh, she turned to the scans, running her eyes over them herself. 'No sign of any abnormalities.'

'This time,' Mark said, with a pointed note to his voice that made her flinch.

'Mark—' Emma started, but he raised his hands in defence before she could continue.

'I'm sorry. I said I was going to drop it and I will.' He got up from his chair and stepped closer to her, so she had to tilt her head to keep looking at him. 'I just worry about you.'

Don't, she wanted to say, but the word refused to cross the boundaries of her lips. Worry wasn't something that worked in the confinements of this affair they'd created. Concern implied something more substantial than she could permit in her life. Besides, he had been clear that he wasn't ready for anything beyond a physical relationship. She'd be foolish to believe otherwise.

His head dipped, his mouth brushing over her lips in the soft suggestion of a kiss. 'Let's go and get your blood drawn.'

Mark stepped away from her, and the void he left between them rushed into her awareness as a yearning unlike the one she'd experienced over the last week swept through her body. Its roots lay in comfort rather than desire, and it filled her with a gentle, cosy warmth.

She pushed those emotions away and followed him through the door into an exam room, where he sat her down on the table as he put on gloves.

'You good?' He looked at her, his dark brown eyes still sparkling with the same concern that had driven him to demand to take her to the hospital straight away.

Emma watched as Mark drew her blood, all too familiar with the sight. 'Can you file this under Jane Doe? I don't want it to cause any trouble, should anyone hear about my blood being tested.'

'Sure. I was thinking the same thing—for the sake of your own privacy as well.'

He shook the vial, to make sure the blood

mixed with the anti-coagulant, and pressed a piece of cotton wool against the injection wound. They sat there for a moment, his thumb pressing against the crook of her elbow while his other hand grazed over the inside of her hand in a reassuring motion.

'This will take a while, so we might want to think of something to do.' He looked at her, a mischievous grin curling his lips.

Emma laughed and rolled her eyes at him. 'We are in the hospital, Dr Henderson. Get your mind out of the gutter. I can list ten reasons why that is a terrible idea.'

He placed a plaster on the injection site and released her arm. 'Is that so?'

'One: while it's not specified in the employee handbook, it's implied that staff need to be clothed at all times. Two: I'm only here on a short-term contract, which can be dissolved at any moment. Three: have I mentioned this is a hospital?'

Mark interrupted her by standing up from his stool and towering over her, forcing her to tilt her head all the way back. His hands wove through her hair, pulling her face closer to his as he wrapped her in an indulgent kiss full of promise and potential.

Emma sighed, melting against him and forgetting every word she had just said. The spark of desire and the longing to give in to his suggestion cascaded through her and mingled with something else—an unbidden sprouting of deep affection for the man standing in front of her.

That affection would prove her undoing, something within Emma whispered, loudly enough for the meaning of the words to pierce her consciousness.

What if she got sick? How would that affect them? She could not let this kind of misguided affection take root in her heart. He'd been clear about his expectations of their fling...had even shown her the damage his wife's fate had left within him. Not only that, but Emma was headed to a place he refused to go.

With greater effort than she wanted to admit, she moved back out of reach of his lips and took a deep breath. 'You are trying to get me into trouble at this point.' Her voice sounded a lot more playful than she felt, and to her relief Mark stepped back, so she didn't have to rely on her sense of self-preservation alone. Because she knew if that was what it came to she would be in deep trouble.

'You're right, of course,' he admitted with a one-sided smile. He grabbed the vial and placed it in a transparent bag which he labelled 'Jane Doe'. 'Care to walk me to the lab?'

They walked in comfortable silence, and her

thoughts wandered enough that she didn't notice they'd arrived at the lab until an intern approached her.

'I didn't realise you were already here. I've got the scans from Mrs Williams ready, if you want to have a look.'

Emma furrowed her brow as her brain found its way back to reality, but Mark turned around beside her, looking at the intern. 'Let's see what we're working with here. Can you bring me a tablet loaded with the scans? We'll take it from there.'

The intern nodded, and only then did Emma catch up. 'Oh, Georgina's scans.' She frowned as she noted the time. 'It took her longer than I would have expected to be stable enough for a scan.'

Mark nodded, his grim expression a reflection of her own thoughts on the prognosis of this patient.

The intern brought the tablet, and Mark motioned Emma to follow him to his office, where he sat down behind his desk to look at the scans.

Emma moved around the desk so she could watch over his shoulder, the hair on her arms rising at her proximity to him. She squeezed her eyes shut for a moment, willing her thoughts away as she reminded herself that bigger things were at stake right now.

'There's nothing there,' he said, and sighed. They stared at the scans, each of them following their own diagnostic thoughts. 'I wonder if the chemotherapy shrank any metastasis before it became visible. Though that doesn't explain her heart failure, or her deteriorating health. She seemed fine last week.'

He swore under his breath, and for a moment Emma thought he might throw the tablet across the room. But he laid it down on the desk instead, burying his face in his hands. He was more tense than usual. She could see the strain this case had put on him was higher than with other cases they'd collaborated on. She thought of Georgina and Harald and their circumstances. Did the case remind him of his own struggles as a spouse?

'What can we do?' Emma picked up the tablet to look at the pictures again.

Mark sat up at the question, his eyes veiled with deep thoughts. 'We could go for another lymph node dissection. The first one didn't come back negative—it was inconclusive. The surgery itself is not as taxing if we go through a keyhole, although her body has already been through a lot at this point. I'm worried about what another surgery might do to her.' He sighed again, with a frown. 'I don't think she can stand any more radiation. Her condition is a lot more critical than I expected.'

A shadow flickered across his face. A well of pain was clearly springing to life within him. Emma got a glimpse of it for the duration of a heartbeat before his expression shuttered.

'Are you okay?' she asked. She wanted to understand the pain he was hiding from her, despite knowing it would be better if she didn't.

'I'm fine.'

The shortness of his answer hurt more than Emma cared to admit. He clearly wasn't fine, and while it was better for their entanglement if he didn't lean on her for emotional support, she found she wanted him to anyway. And she knew just what to do.

'Her oncologist won't be here until later. Let me take you somewhere before we plan Georgina's surgery.'

'Somewhere' wasn't far from his office. They didn't have to go very far before they reached their destination.

Emma twirled around in the greenhouse on the roof of the hospital. The founder of the hospital had enjoyed the cultivation of medicinal herbs so much that he'd made it a permanent fixture. Mark had never been up here—his department needed a lot stronger medication than plants could yield—though he knew Emma had enjoyed some time up here among the plants for her own leisure.

Unsurprising, he thought, as he remembered how fond she had been of the flower garden in the park. However, Mark wasn't sure why she had brought him here now. Georgina's vitals were steady at the moment, but they weren't within a range that made him confident about performing surgery on her.

A strange desperation gripped him whenever he thought of her case, and a feeling of inadequacy clung to his heart with her every turn for the worse. Many patients had died before, and he knew he couldn't save everyone. But this had become a lot more personal than it should have, unearthing old insecurities that he'd thought he had left behind.

He hadn't been able to save Claire, and in trying he had made her suffer so much more than if he had admitted that he couldn't. Mark had been absent, driven by the wrong motivation. He hadn't wanted to lose her, but they had reached the point of no return. He had ignored that, instead focusing on forestalling the inevitable so he wouldn't feel the pain he'd seen barrelling towards him.

Georgina and her struggles had brought those

memories back, confronting him with a time of his life when he'd been at his lowest.

And then there was Emma.

She led him by the hand through the greenhouse, stopping now and then to show him an interesting plant before moving on. Her presence calmed him, but now he felt something else. She might be sick, too.

Mark had no right to feel deceived, yet that was one of the emotions battling for prominence inside his chest. They weren't a couple. He had established that firm boundary himself. She was under no obligation to tell him something that personal. Yet it still disappointed him that Emma hadn't. He had shared so much with her—much more than he had with any other person. It hurt to think she didn't have the same trust in him.

They'd arrived at the far end of the greenhouse. To Mark's surprise, he was staring at a cushioned swing bench.

'I'm not the only one who likes to seek refuge in here. It's very calming to be around plants,' Emma said, and sat down on the bench. 'I figured you needed some time away from your office to clear your head. Is Georgina's case getting the better of you?'

'Among other things,' he mumbled without thinking, and he scrubbed his hands over his face, feeling the strain of the last couple of hours draining all his remaining energy.

'Ah…' Emma breathed, noticing the subtext in his short answer. 'You think I should have told you about my potential diagnosis earlier?'

Mark looked up, searching his mind for an answer that wouldn't come. He opened his mouth, only to be interrupted by Emma waving her hand.

'Let's try something before we continue this conversation. We have a hard day ahead of us, so we need to feel fresh.' She moved to the far side of the bench and patted her thighs. 'Lie down here for a couple of moments.'

'On your lap?' Mark raised an eyebrow, unable to remove the scepticism from his voice.

'Just try it. If you don't like it I will release you.'

Emma indicated her lap again with an encouraging smile until Mark relented, lying down on his side until his head came to a rest on her thighs.

The sweet scent of coconut drifted up his nose, mingling with the fresh aroma of the herbs being cultivated in the greenhouse. He closed his eyes for a moment as he stretched out on the bench, his thoughts coming to a rest for the first time in hours.

Emma laid one hand on his shoulder while

the other one ran through his hair, her fingers playing with the strands as she caressed his scalp. A deep sigh left his chest as each muscle in his body relaxed, one after the other. He didn't know how long they lay like that, with her fingers gently scratching his head, until Emma spoke again.

'Georgina's condition must hit close to home.' Her fingers didn't stop their caress, easing some of his stress. 'Do you feel you should be doing more?'

'No, I've done everything I should.' His voice sounded hollow. Those were words he had said to himself before.

'Does she remind you of Claire?'

Emma's words came out with a hint of hesitation. Was she uncertain whether she wanted to know? Did he even want to talk about this? Her hands felt so reassuring and calming. He didn't want to leave the warm bubble behind. But he sensed a disconnect within him—a myriad of emotions clashing with each other and brewing up a storm inside of him.

Georgina did remind him of Claire, of his loss and his failings. But, even more, Emma reminded him of how pain had almost destroyed him.

'She does,' he said. 'But so do you. A lot more

than Georgina.' He paused for a moment, releasing a deep breath.

'I didn't know how to tell you,' she said. 'Not after hearing what you went through with Claire. I was afraid of how you would react to my wilful ignorance.'

She spoke from somewhere above him. He shifted around so he could look up at her. The fear in her eyes was something he was too familiar with. He had lived with the same terror for a long time.

His heart had almost fallen out of his chest as he'd waited for the results of Emma's scans to load up. An enormous sigh of relief had fallen from his lips when they'd come back clean. Mark had become a lot more attached to Emma than he should have allowed himself to. But the ghosts of the past still lived in his heart. He had failed to fulfil one of the most important promises he had made in his life.

In sickness and in health.

'This place has become important to me.'

The wistful tone of her voice drew his attention back to her, and he looked up to find her eyes with his. The emotion shining in them made his heart slam against his chest.

'This greenhouse?'

It was an obtuse question, but Mark needed something to deflect the truth he saw written in her face. She must not admit to feelings for him. They just couldn't go there.

'Yes, the greenhouse as well. It's been a haven when things are overwhelming. The scent of earth and petrichor reminds me of the time we went on holiday to the rainforest. I wanted to see a jaguar, but all we ever spotted were some bush rats.' Emma laughed at the memories, before falling quiet again with a contemplating look. 'But I meant Chicago. I didn't plan on getting attached to this place. But things changed. You changed them for me. We became something I never expected, and I…'

Her voice trembled, and Mark watched her swallow, as if there was a heavy lump in her throat. His pulse quickened, feelings of both warm affection and icy dread welling up in him. They weren't allowed to go there. Emma was leaving for the Whitebridge Institute, where she would do extraordinary things. It was the place where he had laid all his demons to rest, before turning his back on it for ever.

She might want to give it up for him, knowing he wouldn't set foot in this place again. But Mark didn't want to create a situation where she would feel compelled to choose one thing over another. He wasn't a person worthy enough to warrant such a sacrifice. Just as he couldn't put himself in a situation where he had to be a doctor and the spouse of a sick person at the same time.

The last time had broken him irrevocably. He couldn't let Emma go on with that sentence. 'Nothing has changed. This isn't more than two people enjoying each other's company.' The words he'd spoken turned to ash in his mouth and he swallowed the bitterness, not wanting it reflected in his expression.

Emma's hands stopped moving, and he felt her body stiffen under his head. 'What? A moment ago you were upset at me for not telling you about my condition sooner, and now you're telling me you don't care about me?'

The intimacy of the moment broken, Mark sat up to look at her. 'We're doctors. We should know these things about ourselves—which is why I pushed you to get scanned. How are you going to advocate for your patients when you can't face the truth yourself?'

Emma looked as if he'd struck her, her eyes wide in disbelief at his words. He'd regretted them the moment he said them, knowing that they did not convey everything he wanted to tell her. That she too had become important to him over the last couple of weeks.

He stood as if at the edge of a cliff, ready to fall for her but too terrified of what he saw beyond the cliff to move. It might be blissful happiness. Or another wave of unending heart-break.

Mark couldn't tell her. The likely chance was that they were looking at the latter of those two things.

Emma stood, taking a few steps away from him towards a winding plant that was climbing its way up a trellis. Her hands were balled into tight fists hanging by her sides.

'I guess I was wrong about you,' she said eventually as she turned to face him again, her expression shuttered and unreadable.

Mark got to his feet with a sigh, feeling a pain stab through his chest that made it hard to breathe. He hesitated for a moment, unsure if he should explain himself any further or if the decision had been made for him. His hand hovered in the air as he thought about wrapping her in his arms. If this was to be the last time, he wanted to remember it. But he knew he would only make things worse by giving in to his self-ish need for one last touch.

'I should check on Georgina,' he said, with a last look at Emma.

She had her back turned towards him, stiff as she processed what had happened between them. Her hand was touching a large, waxy leaf on the plant she stood in front of.

If there was such a thing as a good place to

have this conversation, it was this one, Mark thought with a rueful smile. She would soon realise that he wasn't worth the heartache and live her best life away from him.

Those were the thoughts Mark leaned on as he left her in the greenhouse, struggling to cope with his own broken heart.

CHAPTER TEN

THE NEXT COUPLE of days went by agonisingly slowly, but at the same time the hours seemed to be just flying by for Emma. The end of her contract was fast approaching. Soon she would have to pack up her life again and move to Rochester, finally starting her fellowship at the Whitebridge Institute. The moment she had been looking forward to since reading her acceptance letter.

Only now a heavy sense of regret had mixed itself into her excitement, bringing a bitter taste to her mouth. She was due to leave soon, and the connection between her and Mark had already all but fallen apart.

How had she ended up in the situation she'd told herself to avoid the second she'd laid eyes on him? The rules had been clear from the start. She wasn't to fall for her boss again.

Now that was the only thing occupying her mind.

She wanted Mark.

The rules, boundaries and walls she had drawn around her had done next to nothing to protect her heart from this incredible man. The moment they'd met, Emma hadn't been able to resist him. She'd let her guard down, and now she was paying for it.

The meetings between them since that day in the greenhouse had been tense, neither of them willing to mention what had happened.

How could she have been so close to confessing her love to him, only for him to pull away from her? It had just been about sex for him. The thought crushed her almost as much as his rejection, and she couldn't believe that her brain had misled her.

Words were one thing, but the concern he had shown when he'd learned she might be sick had convinced her that there might be more. That he might feel the same way. A silly, misguided notion, Emma now knew. He had been worried about one of his doctors being sick, not about her. He wasn't worried about losing her, because she meant nothing to him.

Emma shook those thoughts away as she wrapped up in the OR. This was her last surgery with this particular team, so she made her farewells to everyone on staff. Christine, the department's anaesthetist, had already returned to work, so Emma had handed over most of her active cases. The only one left was Georgina.

She had grown so close to the woman that she wanted to see her case through until her very last day. Even though that meant having Mark in her space.

A hot spear of hurt pierced her chest every time she saw him in the corridors, along with a sense of deep longing and affection. The feelings remained no matter how much she told herself that this was for the best. She should never have fallen for him in the first place.

With a sigh, Emma approached the nurses' desk and grabbed a tablet to check on Georgina's notes before she went into surgery in a couple of hours. They'd scheduled a full lymphadenectomy as her scans had once again come back inconclusive. Despite her fragile state, an exploratory surgical procedure remained their best option.

'You look glum,' Theresa said from behind the counter, catching Emma's attention.

'This is going to be my last surgery here. After this I'll hand over Georgina's case to your permanent anaesthesiologist.'

That wasn't the true reason for her gloomy mood, but it was plausible enough not to raise any suspicion. Though Emma hadn't counted on the well-connected head nurse.

'What? No, you can't leave yet. Not before you patch things up with Mark.'

Theresa's words made her feel as if someone had poured a pitcher of iced water into her veins, spreading a chilly shiver throughout her body.

'What? We didn't—'

Theresa waved her hand in front of her, dismissing any further objections. 'Please don't insult me by lying to me. I know everything that goes on in my department.'

'How could you possibly know?' Emma was in shock. If Theresa knew about their affair, how far had it spread in the hospital?

As if reading her thoughts, the head nurse shook her head. 'You weren't exactly subtle, with the way you were tiptoeing around each other, but don't be too worried. It's just us nurses who pay enough attention to notice something like that. You doctors are way too self-absorbed.'

Emma breathed a sigh of relief, though the sensation didn't last long when she looked at Theresa. 'Well, whatever it was, it's over now. He's made that clear.'

'I struggle to believe that. He was so reserved when he first started, but that changed after you arrived. There's no way he doesn't have feelings for you.'

A confusing heat ignited under her skin, mingling with the chill she had felt just moments ago. Mark had feelings for her? No, that wasn't possible. He had stopped her confessing her affection for him. Why would he have done that if not because he didn't love her? Or had she misread the situation?

Her thoughts were interrupted when the target of her contemplations arrived at the nurses' station. He glanced at Theresa for a moment, before turning to her.

'I've updated Georgina's surgical plan after consulting with the oncologist. You can find it in her file.'

Emma nodded, not daring to open her mouth. She searched his face for the same stabbing pain she felt in her chest, but his expression remained flat. Unyielding.

'I think you're wrong,' Emma said as she looked at Theresa before letting her gaze go back to Mark. 'I'll see you in the OR, Dr Henderson.'

Mark stood over Georgina, looking down at the incision site with his fingers wrapped around his scalpel. The way he'd planned the surgery, he'd put the scalpel on her skin and make a small incision right on her armpit, not much larger than the span between his fingertip and the second knuckle. Through the small opening, the resident surgeon assisting him would feed a small tube-shaped camera that would be their guide.

Mark himself inserted a long, staff-like instrument with a sharp claw at its end into the keyhole. His eyes left the patient and fixed on the monitor at his eye level to find their way to the lymph nodes. They were located close to the surface, so neither of the two instruments had to go far before they got to their goal and started extracting the lymph nodes.

They were just finishing up the first half of the lymph node extraction when a sharp beep demanded their attention.

Mark looked at Emma.

'Blood pressure is dropping,' she said, standing up from her stool, her creased eyebrows the only thing visible on her otherwise masked face. 'It's not a reaction to her anaesthesia.'

'Get me the portable ultrasound right now,' he barked at the resident standing next to him. He hurried to retrieve the small machine from one of the storage cases on the far side of the OR.

A drop in blood pressure could only mean blood loss somewhere. Scanning the screen in front of him, Mark could see that there was no bleeding where they had been working, so the cause must be located somewhere else.

The intern handed him the ultrasound, and

Mark moved the gown from the patient's neck, rubbing some gel on her skin before placing the transducer on her shoulder.

The machine came alive with a whirring noise as he moved it around the other side of the armpit and down her ribs, finding no free-flowing liquid. Mark listened to the updates on her vital signs while he moved over to her chest. That was where he found the source of the loss of blood, and he swore.

'There must be a tear somewhere along her aortic artery.' He looked up at one of the assisting nurses. 'Page someone from Cardio—we need to have an expert in here. You.' He looked at the resident, who was still holding the camera in place. 'Prep her chest. We're going to open her up to look at the aorta.'

While the resident worked fast to change the surgical field, Mark removed the camera and instruments they were working with before stepping up with a fresh scalpel.

'Heart-rate's dropping.'

Emma's distant voice altered him. If he could get to the heart fast enough, he could keep her alive until the cardiac surgeon arrived.

But Mark was not prepared for the devastation that he encountered there, and his years of training as a surgeon told him that there was nothing he could do to fix that kind of damage.

The walls of the aorta had ruptured, weakened from the ongoing stress her entire body was under. Georgina had fought, but in the end they were going to lose her.

Emma picked up on his hesitation, stepping forward to look at the surgical field. 'What do you want to do?' she asked as he stood there, looking defeat in the eye.

'There's nothing we can do. The damage is too big.'

His voice sounded hollow, and the edge to it surprised him. He had been in this place many times before. People came to this hospital from all over the country after they had exhausted their first and second opinions. But with his stellar reputation came the drawback: the saw the hardest cases, so he lost as many patients as he saved.

This case had been different from the very start. Despite his experience as a doctor, he'd got attached to Georgina and Harald. Their situation was so hauntingly familiar to his own with Claire. Right down to this moment now, where he couldn't save her.

By the time the cardiac surgeon arrived Mark had already declared the time of death. One look at the scene before her made the heart surgeon come to the same conclusion.

'She was in danger before she got on your

table, Dr Henderson,' she said to reassure him, as he instructed the residents to close the patient up.

Now he had to go and talk to Georgina's husband about what had happened. A conversation he'd had so many times in the past.

In his specialty Mark had learned early on to untangle himself from his patients so he could cope with the emotion. Plenty of doctors ended up choosing different specialties for that precise reason, yet for him it had always been a point of strength to comfort people in their time of need. But at this moment, as he walked out of the operating room, he felt a paralysing fear grip him as the darkness came rushing back at him.

No matter how hard he fought to save his patients, redemption for his past failings seemed out of his grasp. He would always be the man defined by the mistake he'd made with the person who had depended on him the most.

'Mark, wait.'

Emma's voice made him stop mid-stride.

'Let me come with you.'

'I don't need your help to talk to a patient's husband.'

The hurt flickering over her expression for a mere second pulled a tight string around his chest, making him regret the lack of control over his tone.

'I'm sorry.'

'It was a rough surgery.'

She closed the distance between them, grabbing his hand and squeezing it for a moment before letting it go. The warmth of her touch lingered on his skin, shining a faint light into the dark fog inside him. He could sense relief for a moment, a yearning for the short reprieve to be permanent. But he didn't dare to get used to it or it would prove his undoing.

She had awoken something in him he'd believed long dead, and the thought of examining that something more closely sent pangs of terror through his chest. He'd let their affair go too far, and now he was fighting an internal battle on how to take it back.

Emma had been brilliant, filling his plagued soul with life and laughter. She'd shown him there was still hope for him when he'd believed it all gone. But was he strong enough to go through all this again?

Doubt clawed at his heart, reaffirming the decision he'd made several days ago to distance himself from her. The thought of losing her down the line, of having to bear the weight of the entire world on his shoulders again, filled him with a cold anxiety that kept him up at night.

Mark hated to admit it, but if he hadn't been

strong enough back then, how could he be strong enough now? Emma deserved someone who could carry her all the way, no matter what the ending looked like.

'I'll go and inform Harald about the surgery.'

The same news that Mark himself had heard two years back. Words he had delivered to patients countless times without his own chest feeling tight with the pressure of anxiety. Nothing should be different this time around. But something inside him had shifted, making announcing the outcome of this surgery almost unbearable.

Gritting his teeth, Mark swallowed the anxiety spreading through his chest as he approached Harald, who was waiting in Georgina's room for news about his wife.

Georgina's death shook the entire oncology department when news of the surgery spread.

Emma stood at the nurses' station, filling out the paperwork both Mark and Harald would need to sign.

Emma's heart went out to both men. Mark liked to seem detached with his patients, hiding behind the professional distance he put between himself and his cases. But she knew the bad outcome of this one had impacted him. Everyone had fought so hard to keep Georgina alive.

Emma sighed, picking up the piece of paper and starting the walk to Mark's office. She wanted to drop the paper by his desk and then leave this place behind.

A small voice within her urged her to check in on Mark, to make sure he was okay, even though she wasn't sure he even wanted to see her. His nerves must have been shot after the surgery. But he had never snapped at her like that. Could it be that he really didn't care for her at all?

Emma pushed those thoughts away as she knocked on his door before opening it.

Mark sat on the couch, his face briefly lifting to see who entered. When he saw her, his expression softened, and he let himself slump backwards with a heavy sigh on his lips.

Emma put the paper on his desk before sitting down next to him, leaving a hand span of space between them. They sat there in sombre silence for a few heartbeats, each one chasing their own thoughts about today's events.

Emma grew more tense, the uncertainty between them wrapping itself around her shoulders and chest, making each breath harder than the last. Would he reject her offer of comfort and ask her to leave?

She knew they weren't on good terms, but they had both lost a patient they'd been working with since she'd first started there. Despite their very painful relationship, she couldn't leave him without another word when Georgina's death had impacted him so much.

As if sensing her tension, Mark reached out and pulled her into his arms without a single word. Her head came to rest on his shoulder and she felt his warmth seeping through her skin, reminding her of a time when things had been simpler.

His chin rested on the top of her head as his fingers trailed up and down her spine, leaving tiny goosebumps as they went. She wanted nothing more than to enjoy being in his arms once more, to let herself be carried away by his touch the way she had in the last couple of weeks. But she couldn't trust his intentions. Hadn't he rejected her just a couple of days ago?

'Mark…' she whispered, and felt his arms around her tighten.

'I broke an important promise,' he said in a quiet voice.

She twisted out of his arms to look at him. 'What? You didn't promise Harald and Georgina a good outcome.'

She tried to catch his eye, but Mark kept on staring ahead, deep in thought.

'No, I broke my promise to Claire. I promised to be there for her, but when the time came I couldn't do it.'

He moved away from her, burying his face in his hands. Emma laid her hand on his back. She'd come here to comfort him—one last act of affection before she left him and this city behind for ever. Only she didn't want to walk away if there was a chance for them. In all her life she had never felt so connected to another person that it had changed her life in a profound and meaningful way. She knew she was in love with Mark.

Maybe Theresa was right, and he felt something, too. He had been the one to break things off, but in this moment, when he was vulnerable, he leaned on her.

'What happened?' she asked when he remained silent.

'Claire... She was getting better. But her oncologist was still cautious, warning us that it might just be a second wind. I knew that, of course, and I'd seen it myself in so many patients. After seeing her scans, as a doctor I should have told myself to prepare for the worst. I knew that—and yet I didn't. Instead of being there for her as she deteriorated I was in the lab, chasing an impossible cure, when I knew full well I was decades away from any results.'

Mark's voice was calm, but Emma felt his

muscles tense under her touch. He still carried so much guilt around when he had reacted little differently from any other spouse—clinging to hope, however unlikely it was.

'You tried to fight it your own way,' she told him. 'Some family members do little more than sit there and pray while the doctors do their best to make a good outcome happen. You were different, having an entire research department at hand. It's only natural that you'd seek an answer there.'

Mark lifted his head to look at her, a haunting expression in his brown eyes. 'Maybe that's true. But my mad dash to the finish line was no more than a distraction. The woman I married was fading away in front of my eyes, and I couldn't be there for her. I got distracted, wanting to save myself the pain of losing her rather than paying her attention in her last days.'

It was something Emma understood well. It had been one of the hardest things to watch her mother grow weaker every day. Some days it had been too much to sit by and watch her suffer. In those times she'd had to look no further than her family. They'd made sure her mother was never alone while she and her father got some space to mend themselves.

'You were all by yourself?' Emma asked, to confirm her suspicion.

Mark looked puzzled for a moment, as if he didn't understand the relevance of the question. 'It was just me and her.'

'No wonder you struggled. The death of a spouse is one of the toughest times in many people's lives—especially when you have to deal with it all alone. Haven't you noticed how many people our patients surround themselves with?'

Emma paused for a moment. She wanted to reach out to him, pull him back into her arms. She had never realised the extent of the hurt he still carried around with him, how much he blamed himself for what had happened.

'My father and I shared the burden with my aunts and uncles, each of us staying with her while the rest looked after ourselves.'

'But I grew distant, anticipating the pain and looking for a way to minimise it,' he said. 'I chose to be selfish.'

His voice sounded brittle, as if he was going to break at any moment. Emma's chest constricted. She was feeling his pain in her own body.

'No, you did what anyone would have done under mounting and unrelenting pressure. You reached the end of your rope. There was no choice but to let go.'

'I…want to believe that's true…' Mark hesitated before looking at her again.

The expression on his face was a mixture of gratitude and the mental anguish he had been putting himself through over the years. And Emma knew he understood everything she'd said to be true. She had heard himself say those things to patients when they were struggling. Harald had been one of those cases where the next of kin didn't have any immediate family for support. But Mark ran a team of compassionate doctors and nurses, who were all willing to step in when any of the over-extended spouses needed a break.

'Is that why you won't admit what I know we're both feeling? Because you want to keep punishing yourself for being human?'

'Emma...' His voice trailed off as he searched for the right words.

'I love you,' she said. 'I tried hard not to fall for you, but that turned out to be harder than I expected. You are a good and kind man, who deserves to be happy.'

She had to say it or she would regret it for ever. If there was even the whisper of a chance that what she sensed between them was true, she needed to know she'd tried.

Her life was complicated, and the addition of a potential Gardner Syndrome diagnosis made it so much harder. The last thing she wanted was to inflict the same anguish on him again. But it wouldn't be the same. Her family would surround him—*their* family—and they would help him get through it. Wouldn't that be worth the happiness they could find with each other?

The burdens of his past which he had been carrying around for the last two years were lifted from his shoulders. He had never thought to confide in anyone until this moment, too troubled by his failings. But to his own surprise he felt lighter, more at peace with his memories.

Emma's hands were still on his chest, keeping him grounded as her sparkling green eyes encouraged him to bare his soul to her. And Mark noticed that he wanted to. For years he had been the bearer of his own memories, fighting off anyone who stepped too close to him. Thinking that he didn't deserve kindness or love ever again—not after breaking the most important promise he had ever made. He wasn't trustworthy, and as penance he had thought he must carry the guilt of it around for the rest of his life.

Until Emma had appeared in his life just a few weeks ago.

But when she'd said those words—the ones he'd imagined her saying in the dead of night as he'd watched her drift off to sleep—a thrill of terror entered his chest.

He got up from the couch abruptly, crossing the room in long strides to put some distance between them. Raking his hands through his hair, he looked up to the ceiling as he tried to find his composure. Deep down in his heart he wanted to say it back. He loved her too. But fear struck hard, much harder than he'd imagined, drowning out everything else in him.

'I can't do this again,' he said with a lump in his throat, and he looked at Emma.

A torrent of hurt engulfed her eyes. 'Because I could be sick? That's the reason you're going to deny everything that's gone on between us?'

Mark shook his head, trying to make sense of the onslaught of different feelings rising within him. Her words from earlier rang in the air, and he searched their meaning for truth. Despite hearing about all his demons, and knowing how he had failed Claire, Emma was ready to forgive him.

But was she ready to put the same kind of trust in him? How long would she have kept that secret to herself? He couldn't help but wonder, and the small voice in the back of his head whispered those words in his ear.

'You didn't tell me you were sick until I stumbled upon the information myself.' His eyes snapped back to her as he crossed his arms in front of his chest. 'Would you even have told me if I hadn't confronted you about it?'

Emma swallowed, pale under her usually tanned skin as she took his words in. 'You must know that's an impossible question to answer. I didn't think I would fall for you, so I didn't think it would be necessary to talk about it. The plan was for me to leave without you.'

His jaw felt tight, and Mark took a few breaths to relax, though the exercise did precious little to calm his inner turmoil. 'After everything you knew about me, you kept it from me. How did you see that playing out?'

'Why are you acting like you're entitled to know every detail of my medical history?' Emma got to her feet as well, her hands balled into fists by her sides. Her eyes narrowed to a glare. 'You were the one who told me this was only a physical relationship. I don't tend to share that kind of information with men I don't mean anything to.'

Her words hit harder than Mark had anticipated, stabbing a searing pain into his chest. She wasn't wrong. He *had* been the one to insist on a purely physical affair, because he'd wanted to avoid exactly this kind of moment.

'Would you get a genetic test if I asked you to?' He didn't know why he'd asked that question, but he wanted to know. There wasn't anything she could tell him that would convince him that not knowing was better than knowing. He couldn't live in that kind of vacuum—just waiting for the sword above their heads to drop. Though he wasn't sure if he would give them a chance even if she said yes. What if he wasn't strong enough again?

Emma hesitated, a deep frown on her face. She clearly hadn't expected that question.

'I haven't thought that far ahead. Would that change your answer? You need to know whether I'm sick or not to decide if you want to be with me?'

She paused, looking at him with expectant eyes, waiting for him to deny it. Mark stayed silent. Only their breaths were audible.

'That can't be true. That's not the man you are, Mark.'

'Then you don't know me as well as you thought you did.' He had to force the words out of his mouth, and the taste of them turned bitter when her face contorted in pain.

'Mark, I don't do ultimatums. Not any more.'

Her voice sounded hollow, without any of the warmth and affection he had heard just a few moments ago.

'I was stuck for too long, wasting time I didn't have. You either want to be with me or you don't. Whatever a genetic test says shouldn't matter.'

'It's not just your life that hangs in the balance in this situation. You picture it as a black and white question…a yes or no answer. But it goes far beyond that.' He rubbed his hands over his face, his chest constricting with the pain of the words.

'But it is. It's *my* life, and I'm the only one who gets to decide what I'm comfortable with. That's the deal you're buying into if you want to be with me.'

Mark dropped his head for a moment, scrubbing over his hair with his fingers. Terror constricted his chest, pushing the air out of his lungs to the point where it became hard to breathe as history repeated itself in front of his eyes. As much as he regretted it, he knew he wasn't strong enough to withstand another storm.

He shook his head, unable to utter another word.

'You're right. I really don't know you at all.'

Her voice trembled when she said that, and a shaky smile pulled at the corners of her lips as she turned to leave.

The urge to stop her leaving, to wrap her in his arms and never let her go, burned through him, and it took every ounce of self-restraint for Mark to keep his distance.

Emma looked at him for one last glance, a silent plea in her eyes. He dropped his eyes to the floor, releasing the sigh he had been holding in when he heard the door open and close.

CHAPTER ELEVEN

WEEKS HAD PASSED since Emma had left Attano Memorial, and Mark was still waiting for things to go back to the way they were. Each day he woke up thinking things might be easier today, and each day brought a new disappointment.

He missed Emma in the corridors of the oncology department, spreading cheer and compassion among staff and patients alike. He missed her in the OR, where her calm voice had helped him navigate the most difficult surgeries. Most of all he missed her in the part of his heart that had been an open wound since the day she'd left.

His grief over the life he couldn't give her, the life he couldn't permit himself to have, clung to his soul like black tar, making it hard to breathe.

He'd done the right thing, hadn't he?

The nagging question at the back of his mind was the worst part about trying to move on. It struck at him in the quiet moments, when he was trying his best not to think about Emma and how she was doing.

'Mark?'

Theresa's voice jerked him out of his gloomy contemplations. 'Sorry, what were you saying?'

The head nurse raised her eyebrow at him. 'I said hello. Are you okay?'

He looked at her for a couple of breaths. Mark was almost certain that Theresa knew about his feelings for Emma, even though she had never outright said anything.

'One day I hope to be,' he said. He didn't want to lie to her, but the conversation she was trying to start was not one he wanted to have right now. All he wanted was a few quiet moments to grieve for the future he had denied himself. 'I have to go.'

A thought entered his mind as he analysed the inner turmoil he was going through. Grief. That was what he'd felt for the last couple of weeks. Grief over Emma, over their relationship and their future together. It was an emotion he was intimately familiar with.

Mark glanced at his watch. Just a couple of minutes past noon. If they hadn't changed the schedule since he'd last visited, they would start in a couple of minutes. His next surgery wasn't until later in the afternoon, so he had the time.

In a snap decision he went to the psychiatric

floor, to see if the support group for surviving spouses was still meeting at the same time and place where he had first attended meetings on his arrival in Chicago.

A familiar sight unfolded in front of him when he pushed the door open. A bunch of chairs stood in the centre of the room, making a circle so the people sitting down could all face each other. With no empty chairs remaining, Mark moved to one side of the room where they had laid out refreshments, pouring himself a coffee as the meeting started.

When he had first arrived in Chicago he hadn't wanted to hear anything about 'processing' his grief, or the different stages he would go through as he came to terms with his wife's death. But when Theresa had learned that he'd lost his wife she'd asked him to attend, telling him that he might be able to recommend the group to the surviving spouses of patients who were going through a similar experience.

The counsellor there, along with the members of the group, had made him reflect on his actions and his emotions, helping him to unpack most of the issues he'd been dealing with. Despite his initial resistance, he'd ended up attending the meetings for several weeks before stopping.

He'd listened to different people speak, discussing their thoughts and feelings. He'd recognised a lot of their thought patterns in himself when he'd first dealt with the loss of Claire. He'd felt as if he himself hadn't moved on that far, still struggling some days, but on hearing other people discuss their pain he'd realised how far he had come in dealing with his own inner demons. They still lurked in the shadows of his mind, but he had learned to deal with them, their darkness no longer consuming his mind.

After an hour, the group dispersed, some of them moving to his side of the room to grab refreshments. Mark was about to leave when a familiar voice stopped him.

'Dr Henderson. I didn't expect to see you here.'

Harald Williams approached him, stretching out his hand in greeting. The shadows under his eyes were familiar ones. The nights were one of the worst things to deal with. The empty spot in bed a constant reminder of what was missing.

'Mr Williams, what a pleasant surprise.'

Harald showed a weak smile. 'One of your staff members suggested this group to me when I came to pick up Gina's things.'

Mark raised an eyebrow. 'After everything that's happened, I didn't think you would want to set another foot in this place.'

'Why not? I know you did everything you

could to save Gina.' Harald seemed surprised by Mark's suggestion.

'Don't you find it overwhelming to be in the space where she died? Reliving those terrible memories every time you come here?' Mark looked around at the faces of other people, to see if he recognised any of them, wondering if they had all lost someone here at Attano Memorial.

'I prefer to think of the good times we spent here. Like when I gave her a bunch of crazy haircuts as she lost her hair. Or the time I spent reading to her when she was getting her treatment. Gina loved to read, but the chemo left her so drained. I took over, reading aloud to her.' He stopped for a moment as he relieved his memories, a small smile on his face. 'But what are you doing here? Is everything okay with Dr Santos?'

Mark looked at him, his eyes wide in surprise. 'Dr Santos? Oh, no, my wife died two years ago.'

Harald sighed. 'Gina was sure you two were going to make it. She thought you would be happy together.'

'I don't know if I can ever be happy again. Feels like I had my one chance at that and it didn't work out.'

The words left his mouth before could stop them. Something about Harald was strangely disarming, when Mark had never been talkative during the support sessions, preferring to listen to others rather than speak himself.

To his surprise, Harald chuckled. 'You're not going to find happiness if you fight it so hard. Do you think that's what your wife wanted? Gina would have my hide if I let her death bind me to the past. She'd want me to be happy when I'm ready for it.'

When he was ready for it? Was that the struggle he'd been feeling all this time? Was his heart telling him he was ready to take the final step? But how could he know that was what it was?

Harald's words reached him at his very core, with Mark almost gasping as things fell into place within him. He had made a mistake, letting the ghosts of his past prevent him from remembering the good times he had in his marriage.

Despite her illness, he and Claire had spent so much time laughing with each other, cherishing the moments, knowing they were going to be their last ones together. Claire had made him say goodbye every time he left the room—made him swear he wouldn't make her an anchor. She had tried to save him from living a solitary life where he denied himself love in her name because he had promised to be with for ever.

Hadn't he done just that?

They walked out of the room, and Harald waved at him as he left. Mark went back to the oncology department, his thoughts racing as a decision formed in his head.

He'd made a mistake in letting Emma go. Gardner Syndrome, working in Rochester— none of it mattered. They were all just excuses to keep up the self-destructive cycle he had been going through the last two years of his life. His demons weren't attached to a place or a specific memory. He'd let them remain within him.

No more. That pattern ended today. He wanted Emma, and he would fight for her.

He arrived at the nurses' station, where Theresa was still sitting behind the computer. 'Can you page Dr Fremo? He needs to take over the surgery for a while.'

Theresa furrowed her brow. 'What's going on?'

'I need to leave. Page him. I have to know he can take over my patients before I head out.'

Everything within him urged him to get to Rochester as soon as possible. If he left now, he could be there by the evening.

'Okay.' Theresa lifted the phone and dialled Dr Fremo's pager number before hanging up. 'Where are you going?'

Mark hesitated for a moment, not sure how much he wanted to share. The gleam in the nurse's eyes, however, told him she had guessed. 'You know where I'm going.'

A big grin parted her lips. 'You're going to Rochester!'

Theresa reached into the drawer under the table, grabbing something. She tossed it at him, and something heavy and metallic landed in his hands. His car keys.

'Wait—why do you have keys to my car?'

'Just go. I can move things around so our patients are cared for.'

Mark grinned, holding up the keys. 'We're going to have a conversation about this, Theresa,' he said, before he turned around and hurried to his car, praying that he hadn't wasted too much time.

Emma sighed when she looked out of the window. The sun had set a couple of hours ago, but she was nowhere near ready to leave. Her apartment contained little comfort outside of the plants she had brought with her. She'd rather distract herself with work.

The few weeks she had spent at the Whitebridge Institute so far had been an eye-opening experience. The brightest medical minds of the country were at her disposal, teaching her everything she needed to know about emergency medicine.

Her switch in specialties was a jarring one that kept Emma on her toes. Her patient care was a lot more hands-on now, requiring her to work more with patients and general medicine. It was a challenge she relished. But it came with its own unique set of stumbling blocks. The most painful one being her broken heart.

When she'd left Attano Memorial that evening, nothing had prepared her for the devastating heartbreak. It had left her numb, and she'd barely managed to put her life together once more and move up here.

But, despite her sadness over how things had ended between her and Mark, she wasn't sad that it had happened. She wanted to be with him. Her entire body ached with the longing for his warm embrace. But deep down within her she understood his hesitance. It hurt, but she knew she came with a lot of baggage. And, as much as her heart was bleeding inside her chest, the affair with Mark had helped her realise a lot of things about herself.

One of them being that she needed to know her diagnosis. Today.

Life was short, even without the possibility of a terminal disease hanging over her head. She wanted to have fun, to travel the world, to fall in love. To do that she needed to know what was going on inside her body, no matter how much it might scared her. Whatever the result might be, she wanted to be in charge of her future.

So now Emma sat in one of the exam rooms in the ER. On the table in front of her spread out were a couple of cotton swabs, some vials containing different liquids, and a syringe to draw her blood. Despite the pain his memory caused her, she knew she had to thank Mark for her newfound courage.

Emma had picked up the first cotton swab, rolling it over her arm to prepare herself for the blood draw, when a knock on the door interrupted her.

'What is it?' she asked, irritation colouring her voice. She had waited until she was sure she was alone to do this.

An intern poked her head into the exam room. 'There's someone here to see you.'

Emma raised her brows. 'Who is it?'

The intern shrugged. 'Don't know him, but it looks like a new doctor's starting here.'

A new hire? Making the rounds this late at night?

'Tell him to come back tomorrow. I'm done with my shift for today.'

The intern vanished and Emma tied the band around her arm, rolling up her sleeve as she balled her hand into a fist to help her find a suitable vein.

'Oh, don't worry about it. She won't mind. She's going to marry me, though she doesn't know that yet.'

The familiar voice sent hot and cold showers down her spine.

'Sir, I really can't…' she heard the intern say.

But a moment later Mark stood in the exam room, all tall and handsome just like she remembered. He smiled at her, a smile full of affection and care, and then his eyes darted downwards, looking at her arm.

'What's happening? Are you okay?'

But before Emma could say anything, still stunned by his sudden appearance, Mark nodded knowingly and was soon sitting down and pulling gloves over his hands. He took the syringe out of her hand. When he'd finished drawing her blood, disposing of the used needle and gloves, she finally found her voice again.

'What are you doing here?' she said, her voice only a whisper. She was still in shock over his sudden appearance.

'I'm here to apologise for how much of a complete idiot I was,' he said as he grabbed the cotton swabs, popping them out of their sterile packaging.

He took one swab and placed his hand on her cheek. His thumb grazed over her lip for a moment before he poked it with his index finger, prompting her to open her mouth. He swished over the inside of her cheeks twice, each time rolling the wooden end of the stick in his fingers. Once done, he unscrewed the plastic vial with the liquid in it, dropping the swab in with the cotton end first. He placed the lid back on top, then put it on the table.

'I was scared of how important you had become to me…how impossible it would be to lose you.'

Mark had lowered his voice. His hand grasped hers, easing her fingers apart so he could weave his through them.

'No, I was wrong to—' Emma stopped when he shook his head, his hand squeezing hers.

'I've realised that this kind of fear has been ruling my life for the last two years, and it took watching you walk away for me to understand how much I was denying myself my true feelings out of fear of pain.' He paused and lifted her hand to his mouth, breathing an airy kiss onto her skin. 'I love you, Emma. I want to be with you. And I don't care what might happen. I know we'll brave anything that comes our way.'

Emma's heart beat against her chest in a near frantic motion, fast enough for her to hear her blood rushing through her ears. He was here. Of all the days he could have picked, he'd come today. When she'd decided to find out the truth once and for all.

Although one thing was burning a hole in her chest. 'But I can't leave here—not now.'

Mark shook his head. 'I came here knowing full well what it meant. It's true that this place holds a lot of my past pain, but that isn't strong enough to hold me back. I'm yours, and if you'll have me I'll move anywhere to be with you.'

Tears stung her eyes, and she blinked a few times. Unable to find the right words to say, instead she stood up from her chair, pulling him from his and wrapping her arms around his neck. He hid his face in her curls, kissing her neck before letting her go long enough so that his mouth could find hers in an indulgent kiss full of all the longing and affection they'd been nurturing for each other.

'I'm so glad you came today,' Emma said when she took a moment to wipe a stray tear off her cheek.

'Are you having another scan?' he asked.

Emma nodded, pressing her head against his chest, finding comfort in the familiar scent of pine that surrounded her. 'Scans to make sure I'm still cancer-free…' She hesitated for a moment. 'And a genetic test to find out whether I have Gardner Syndrome.'

Mark pushed her away from him, his eyes

wide in surprise. 'Are you sure? I don't care what the test says, and I would never ask you to do this for me.'

Emma nodded, her resolve strengthened. 'I'm doing it for me. For us.'

Mark pulled her into another kiss, and Emma melted against his powerful frame. All the worry and the anguish she'd been carrying around fell away from her. Her stomach had turned when she had first recognised his voice as he'd spoken to the intern, but now she felt lighter than she had in weeks.

'Wait—my intern said you're the new doctor working here... And what was that about marrying you?'

Mark chuckled, a wide grin on his face. 'I think we have a few things to talk about.'

Emma's heart sighed as relief washed over her. They both understood the risk. Despite that, he wanted to stand by her. Whatever the result of the test might be, Emma knew she would be okay. Mark would make sure she was.

EPILOGUE

'PAULO, *QUIDADO*!' EMMA flinched as her son came tumbling down the lawn. His cousin sprinted over, pulling the boy back on his feet as they continued their game of *futebol*.

'You worry too much—he's fine. I've heard his mother is a doctor of incredible talent,' said a voice behind her, and Emma looked up.

Mark sat down next to her on the warm stone porch overlooking the back yard of their house on the outskirts of Rio de Janeiro.

They had become Paulo's parents a month ago, after spending the better part of the last year going through the adoption process. Emma's genetic test had come back clean, clearing her of any further prophylactic treatments or scans for Gardner's Syndrome. But despite her clean bill of health they decided to go down the adoption route when they'd met Paulo on their most recent trip to Brazil—a journey they'd taken to get married.

Together they had planned their wedding, opting for a small beach ceremony so the entire Santos clan could attend. One of their guests had told them about the small non-profit clinic he ran in the *favelas*, piquing their interest. Emma's fellowship had been about to end, and they'd started to discussing what to do next. They'd both wanted to do something where they would make a difference.

When they'd gone to see the clinic, a young boy had come in on his own, with a large cut on his upper arm. Emma had spent some time talking to him while she patched him up, and through that conversation she'd learned that he had lost his parents months ago and had since then been living on his own.

That was when they'd both known they wanted to live in Brazil permanently. Their skills were needed, and they had just met their son. Both had known the instant they spoke to him that it was meant to be. Just as *they* were meant to be.

When they'd returned to the States after their wedding they'd wasted no time before arranging their permanent move to Brazil, so they could make their plans for a family a reality.

Emma leaned against Mark with a small smile on her face as she watched the children kick the football around with an abundance of energy and vigour. When she'd taken the test and it had come back negative, a whole new world of possibilities had unfolded in front of her. Things she hadn't dared to dream about had suddenly become a reality because she had known she would be around to see it all through.

And it was thanks to Mark that she'd found the courage to take that step. She'd gone to Chicago to escape the heartbreak of her previous life, not knowing that she was taking the first step in her new life. A life with Mark by her side. He was her rock when she needed him most, pushing her beyond her comfort zone and daring her to grow.

Emma knew that with him by her side nothing bad could ever happen.

* * * * *